She drew in a quick breath and stared at the man blocking her way. Old memories leaped to life and swirled through her mind as she stared at him.

Her tone mocked him lightly. "If it isn't Zane Dantine. What is my uncle's favorite troubleshooter doing in a little mountain town like Ketchum?"

"I want to talk to you about your uncle."

She shook her head. "No dice, Zane. I'm not interested in talking to you or your boss, ever."

She saw him clench his jaw tightly. When he spoke again, his voice had an edge of anger. "When are you going to realize he isn't your enemy?"

She didn't soften. "It's clear to me why you're so quick to defend him, Zane. You're two of a kind—as cold-blooded as they come."

Dear Reader,

Welcome to Silhouette—experience the magic of the wonderful world where two people fall in love. Meet heroines that will make you cheer for their happiness, and heroes (be they the boy next door or a handsome, mysterious stranger) who will win your heart. Silhouette Romance reflects the magic of love—sweeping you away with books that will make you laugh and cry, heartwarming, poignant stories that will move you time and time again.

In the coming months we're publishing romances by many of your all-time favorites, such as Diana Palmer, Brittany Young, Sondra Stanford and Annette Broadrick. Your response to these authors and our other Silhouette Romance authors has served as a touchstone for us, and we're pleased to bring you more books with Silhouette's distinctive medley of charm, wit and—above all—*romance*.

I hope you enjoy this book and the many stories to come. Experience the magic!

Sincerely,

Tara Hughes
Senior Editor
Silhouette Books

BARBARA TURNER

Sister
Wolf

Silhouette *Romance*

Published by Silhouette Books New York

America's Publisher of Contemporary Romance

SILHOUETTE BOOKS
300 E. 42nd St., New York, N.Y. 10017

ISBN: 0-373-08641-5

First Silhouette Books printing April 1989

BARBARA TURNER's

love of romance and happy endings is rooted in the family storytelling and read-aloud sessions of her early childhood in Northern California. Today she lives in San Francisco with her musician husband, one snooty but lovable cat and as many books as she can cram onto bookshelves in every room of her house.

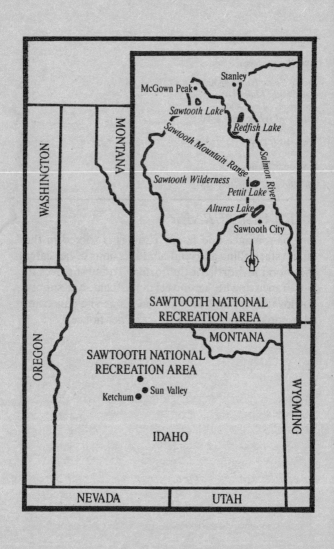

Chapter One

Zane Dantine spotted his quarry moving with un-
hurried grace half a block ahead of him down the
main street of Ketchum, Idaho. Tourists, fishermen,
hunters and locals made up a lively crowd on this
Sunday morning in mid-May, but it wasn't hard to
keep in view the woman he'd traveled four thousand
miles to find. At five foot eight, Jacqui Treherne stood
out in any crowd. Her slenderness and the snug-fitting
jeans and shirt she wore only enhanced the illusion of
height. Sunlight struck gold highlights in the thick
brown braid coiled around her head. A large dog
walked like a gray shadow at her side along the narrow boardwalk that served as a sidewalk in the restored Western town.

She has more than a touch of the old man's pride,
Zane thought, seeing the self-assurance in her stride
and her manner as she greeted some of the local people in passing. Anticipation quickened his pulse. Jac-

qui Treherne at sixteen had been something special,
but now, at twenty-six, she had become a vibrantly
beautiful woman.

For a second, he envisioned her as she'd been the
last time he'd seen her, when she was twenty. Just after her mother's funeral, her face filled with pain and
grief, she'd lashed out at both him and the old man,
crying, "I never want to see either of you again!" But
her tear-blurred gaze had been fixed on Zane.

Now Zane's mouth tightened into a grim line. He'd
backed off six years ago because Jacqui had been
grieving for her mother. But there'd be no backing off
now. His stride lengthened, closing the distance between them on the crowded sidewalk.

A knot of tourists emerged from one of the shops
along the way just as Jacqui was passing. One of the
tourists accidentally shoved too close, and her dog
growled a warning from deep in his chest. Startled, the
man stopped in his tracks and stared down at massive
teeth, fierce eyes and bristling stance. "Hey, lady," he
exclaimed, "what you got there, a wolf?"

Jacqui touched the dog's ruff lightly, and the
threatening growl stopped at once. "Sorry. Buddy was
just letting you know you were crowding us." Her
voice was soft but clear. It had a low, rich timbre that
stirred poignant echoes in Zane's memory.

The tourist hurried away, mumbling that it should
be illegal to keep wolves for pets.

A young woman who was standing in the open door
of a small bookstore nearby waved her hand and called
out, "Jacqui Treherne! I thought Robert said you
weren't due back till June."

"Hello, Susan." Jacqui strolled over. "How's the
bookselling business?"

"We're doing fine," Susan said. "We're staying open year-round now. Between the skiers and the hunters, there's hardly any slow season. Are you back for the whole summer this year?"

"Yes, I'll be trail-guiding with Robert until fall. Want to sign up for a trek into the mountains with us?"

"No, thanks. I'm not much of an outdoor person—all those bugs and snakes! Lordy, I don't think I ever recovered from that time you brought a live rattlesnake to science class." Susan gave a mock shudder and turned back into the shop. "Well, I'd better get back to work ... see you around, Jacqui."

Jacqui moved on, smiling wryly at the memory Susan had stirred. Many of her classmates had taken her deep interest in wild creatures as just one more thing that marked her as "different." *You were right, Gramps,* she thought ruefully. *You said I'd never live down that snake episode.* But she'd been as fierce as a wolf cub then, allowing very few people to get close to her during those first years after her father's tragic death in a mine explosion.

Her steps quickened as she neared a café bearing the sign Marybeth's Kitchen. Inside the café, she hoped to find the one woman who'd seen most clearly the loneliness behind that little girl's defiantly aloof attitude.

"You stay here, Buddy," she ordered, gesturing to a shady spot just outside the café. "I won't be long— I just want to say hello to Marybeth." She went inside, not noticing the man who hesitated, then stopped, as the café's swinging door closed behind her.

Zane leaned up against the hood of a pickup truck parked at the curb. He could afford to wait a while longer, now that he was certain of gaining his goal. He folded his arms across his chest and met Buddy's fixed golden gaze with equanimity. "Don't mind me, Buddy, old boy," he drawled. "We'll both just wait right here for your mistress."

A blast of cool air conditioning hit Jacqui as she entered the café. Except for two fishermen deep in conversation at one end of the counter, the place was empty. A clatter from the kitchen on the other side of the counter made her eyes sparkle with anticipation.

"Hey, back there—how about some service?" There was a lilt in her voice as she called out.

A graying head popped into view in the service pass-through, then blue eyes lit up. "Why, Jacqueline Treherne! Are you back home already?"

Jacqui laughed as she eased her tall form onto one of the high stools at the counter. "I haven't seen you in nearly a year, Marybeth, and you ask 'already?' What kind of welcome is that?"

Marybeth's head disappeared from the pass-through. Seconds later her wide form bustled through the kitchen door. She came around the counter, her face beaming. "You just give me a hug! Of course I'm glad to see you back!"

Jacqui returned the warm embrace and felt a lump form in her throat. She'd had many other hugs from this woman, along with scoldings and praise and understanding. Marybeth had been a second mother to her during a time when she'd needed one. She smiled as Marybeth exclaimed, "I swear you've grown another inch, love. What's up with you? Are you finally through with all your schooling?"

"It's all done but the hard part. I've earned my teaching credential and a degree in wildlife management, but that's no guarantee I'll find a job. I have a few prospects to check out in the fall. How about filling me in on the local gossip? Robert never remembers a thing to tell me except what's happening in the woods."

Marybeth made a clucking sound as she hurried around the counter again to pour two cups of coffee. "Your stepbrother's so closemouthed, you'd think he was the one who had a half-Indian for a grandpa instead of you. But I guess he was bound to pick up on some of Jim Littlewolf's ways, all those summers the two of you spent with the old heathen up in the mountains."

"Now, Marybeth—"

The older woman grinned at her. "You sure do look like your ma when you start pokering up, dearie. You know I always speak whatever comes into my mind. Often enough I told Jim straight to his face that he had no business trying to make Indians out of the pair of you. Teaching you all his mountain tricks, letting you run wild in the woods— Why, every fall when school took up again, the teachers had to civilize you both all over again."

"Robert and I spent the happiest times of our lives with Gramps," Jacqui said defensively. "And Mother wanted us to know both worlds. If she'd been able, she would have gone with us to the mountains herself."

Marybeth nodded her head. Her eyes softened. "Yes, you're just like her—she never could stand for anyone to say a word against your grandpa. Well, you wanted to hear what's going on around here, so..."

They had about ten minutes before their chat was interrupted when the fishermen came to the cash register to pay their check. After the men had gone, Jacqui put down her empty cup and slid off the stool. "Marybeth, it's been great to talk with you, but I'd better be on my way."

Marybeth closed the cash register drawer with a slam. "Where are you headed next? Your steppa's still out of town at that big horse show in Albuquerque."

"I'm on my way up to Robert's cabin. He'll be surprised to see me—he didn't expect me for another two weeks. I plan to use the extra time to roam around a bit on my own before the treks start."

Marybeth shook her head. "You spend too much of your time in the woods and mountains. How do you expect to find a fit mate for yourself? Don't you want to get married and live like normal folks with your own young'uns underfoot?"

Jacqui chuckled as she pushed open the swinging door. "I think I'll stick to my woods and mountains for a while longer, thanks. See you, Marybeth!"

At first Jacqui didn't notice the man waiting near the truck at the curb. She spoke to Buddy, who immediately got to his feet and became her shadow again. But when she turned to go back down the street to her car, her path was barred.

"Hello, Jacqui." Gray eyes as cool and distant as a far mountaintop held hers.

She drew in a quick breath and stared at the man blocking her way. Close to six feet tall, Zane Dantine was only a few inches taller than herself. Yet his presence was enough to hold her rooted. Old memories leaped into life and swirled through her mind as she stared at him. He couldn't be more than thirty-four now, but he looked older, harder than she remembered. His face still had that rawboned look—the look of a man with an unsatisfied hunger. Her gaze dropped to his mouth; it was firmly set, straight and unsmiling. She had other, softer memories of that mouth, but quickly pushed them out of her mind as she came back to her senses.

"Well, well." Her tone mocked him lightly. "If it isn't Zane Dantine. What is my uncle's favorite troubleshooter doing in a little mountain town like Ketchum? I read in the newspapers that Treherne Mining Corporation has a crisis going on in Central America. How on earth are they getting along down there without you to fix things?"

A glint came into his dark gray eyes. "They'll manage. I want to talk to you about your uncle."

She shook her head. "No dice, Zane. I'm not interested in talking to you or your boss, ever. I thought I'd made that clear when I sent back his last letter. So if you'll excuse me—" Stepping to one side, she brushed past him and started up the street. She'd only gone a few steps, however, when he appeared at her side, matching his pace with hers. Buddy whined questioningly.

"If you're thinking of threatening to sic your wolf-dog on me, don't bother," Zane said dryly. "I'm not as easily intimidated as that tourist was."

She slanted a glance at him. "Spying on me, were you? For your information, Buddy's no wolf."

"He looks like one."

"You mean he looks like the popular notion of a wolf." She kept her tone cooler than she felt, and injected a hint of condescension. "Gray wolves, the kind we used to have in Idaho, are usually smaller than

Buddy. Their ears and muzzles are quite different, too, if you're observant enough to notice.''

"When a dog as big as Buddy shows his teeth, what he's called doesn't really matter, does it?''

"You'd do well to keep that in mind.'' She stopped and swung around to face him. "Look, Zane, the only reason Benjamin had for contacting me is finished now. Dad's trust fund has been used up—I'm fully grown, I'm educated. So you can just go back to your boss and tell him there's nothing left for him to administer.''

"Why do you keep referring to him as 'my boss'? Benjamin Treherne is your uncle.''

"That's a technicality I'm not proud of.''

She saw him clamp his jaw tightly. When he spoke again, his voice had an edge of anger. "You may have reached the ripe old age of twenty-six, Jacqui, but when it comes to BJ, you still act the way you did at sixteen. When are you going to realize he isn't your enemy?''

Her eyes narrowed, accentuating her high cheekbones in her triangular face. Her expression gave fleeting evidence of the touch of Shoshone Indian blood in her heritage. "But that's exactly what he is, Zane. My enemy.''

"Dammit, Jacqui, you've never given him a chance. If you really knew him—''

"I can read the newspapers. I know he hasn't changed the kind of man he was, is, and always will be. He's a shark, a destroyer. I want no part of him.''

Zane made a sound of disgust. "BJ has mining interests in some of the political hot spots, so that makes him news, and a lot of it isn't friendly. You can't learn the truth about Benjamin Treherne from newspapers."

She didn't soften. "It's clear to me why you're so quick to defend him, Zane. You're two of a kind—as cold-blooded as they come." She stepped to the curb, looking both ways for traffic without really seeing what she was looking at.

Zane's hard grasp on her elbow halted her, half spun her around, then released her so quickly that Buddy only stared at them both in confusion. "Why can't you admit how far off-base you are about BJ? The last time I saw you, you had an excuse. You were grieving over your mother's death. But what the hell excuse do you have now?"

Jacqui's eyes blazed. "I don't need an excuse to hate him. I knew him long before you ever came on the scene. He destroyed my parents' marriage...my mother's peace of mind...everything. I'll never forgive him for what he did to my family."

"So you're carrying on a vendetta against him?"

"No. He's not worth the energy it would take to square accounts with him. I drew a line between the past and the future six years ago, Zane. Now I'm happy...I have a life I've built for myself, plans for a career. And Benjamin Treherne doesn't come into any of the plans I've made."

"Or me?"

In a voice as cool and steady as his, she replied, "Nor you, Zane. And that's all I have to say."

She turned and stepped out into the street. A car slammed on its brakes noisily, but she ignored the driver's angry shout. She just wanted to put distance between herself and the man she'd once dreamed would become her first—and only—lover.

* * *

Fifteen minutes later, Jacqui pulled her old Chevy to a halt in front of her stepbrother's cabin. Still tense inside from the confrontation with Zane, she yanked the brake on, then jumped out and slammed the car door shut. Buddy went ahead of her on the path and jumped up on the porch, where he flopped down into the shade with a sigh. Jacqui didn't bother to go up to the front door; Robert wouldn't be inside at this hour. She headed around the side of the cabin toward the barn out back.

In the open doorway of the barn, she paused. Her slender height was silhouetted against the sunlight, throwing a shadow inside. A darkly tanned young man seated at a tack bench looked up from the saddle he was mending. He dropped the tool in his hand and started to his feet. His lips formed in a wide grin. "Jacqui! Where'd you come from?"

"From the wilds of Canada, boyo. I tried to phone you to tell you I was coming home early, but kept missing you. How are you, Rob?"

They hugged, then her stepbrother grasped her by the shoulders and held her at arm's length. In a voice that carried a trace of an accent, he exclaimed, "Let me look at you, big sister. I swear you're three inches taller and ten pounds skinnier. What did they feed you on that last field trip up there, moose meat?"

She laughed, but the laugh came out slightly off-key. "I see you haven't been suffering for any lack of good food. You look soft as a pillow." She gave him a mock punch in the stomach.

He winced and let her go. "Don't worry, I'll toughen up once the season gets under way. We've got a full schedule of trips booked this year."

"I hope you haven't got anything booked right away. I could use some time on my own up in the Sawtooths."

Something in her voice must have given her away. Robert took her arm and drew her around so that the light fell more fully on her face. He whistled softly. "Hey, what's happened, Jacqui? Something—or someone—has got you all stirred up."

She shrugged and said, "I stopped in town on my way here. You know it always takes me a little while to readjust to being home again."

He settled back onto the tack bench, keeping his eyes on her face. "Since when could you fool me, Sister Wolf? Better tell me about it."

His use of the Indian name her grandfather had given her made her mouth twist into a reluctant smile. No one but Robert called her that anymore, though she was sure that others, like Susan in town, still thought of her in that role. Eight-year-old Robert Janek, her junior by two years, had been another loner. Recently immigrated from Hungary with his widowed father, he'd entered school in Ketchum and had promptly become a target for bullies. Handicapped by natural shyness and an unfamiliar language, he hadn't been much of a match in school yard battles. Jacqui, always ready to take up for the underdog, had championed him. They'd shared a bond that was strengthened two years later when Anton Janek married her mother.

Now, picking up a riding crop from the tack table, she twisted it in her hands as she paced up and down. Grimly, she said, "I ran into Zane Dantine in town."

"Zane Dantine? The guy who works for your uncle?"

Jacqui threw the crop down again and exclaimed, "I could hardly believe my eyes. After all this time, he just shows up on the street. How on earth did he know I'd be here? I didn't even know till yesterday."

"What did he want?"

She began to pace again. "Something to do with Benjamin, he said. I cut him off before he could tell me any more."

"Aren't you even a little curious?"

There was an odd note in Robert's voice that made her glance at him. "No, I'm not curious. I just want them to stay out of my life for good." She shrugged impatiently. "I don't want to spoil my homecoming even talking about them. I've been looking forward to working with you in the mountains this summer. It'll be the last one for who knows how long."

"Yes, I'm looking forward to this summer, too. But Jacqui, about your uncle—"

She lifted her hand in protest. "Don't, Rob. Let's talk about something pleasant. Like lunch. What have you got in the fridge? I'm starved."

They raided the refrigerator in the cabin and put together a meal of cold venison and leftover vegetables. In spite of her claim to be starved, Jacqui ate sparingly as they caught up on each other's news. They spoke of Anton Janek's chances for success at the big horse show in Albuquerque. Some years before, Jacqui had ridden Anton's purebreds in similar shows, and she felt a nostalgic regret at having to miss this one. Robert questioned her about her experiences on the Canadian field trip, and she teased him about his on-again, off-again courtship of one of the local schoolteachers.

"She'll civilize you, Rob, and about time, too."

A bit red around the ears, he muttered something about clearing up the kitchen and getting back to work. Relenting, she switched to other topics as they dealt with the dishes.

"It feels great to be back home," she declared a few minutes later, swishing a plate through soapy water. "To tell the truth, I was getting a bit fed up with always being the student. Those last few credits I needed seemed to take twice as long as all the rest."

Busy drying a coffee cup, Robert said, "You'd have finished sooner if you hadn't spent half of every year here working for me."

She smiled at him. "It wasn't your fault I decided to take extra courses for my teaching credential. Besides, the money I earned working for you came in handy. My trust fund only paid for the essentials."

He snorted. "I paid you rock-bottom wages, and you were lucky to get that, those first couple of years. You did it to help me keep my guide business from going under, and you know it."

Her grin was flippant but affectionate. "Well, that's what families are for, little brother."

After a troubled glance at her, he cleared his throat. "Jacqui, I know you don't want to hear this, but I have to tell you. I've talked to your uncle."

She stared at him. "You've talked to him? When? Why?"

"He called me yesterday, asking me when I expected you to arrive. He wants to see you. He feels bad that you won't talk to him or answer his letters."

"Sending them back unopened was answer enough."

Robert sighed. "It isn't good, denying your own family."

"The term doesn't fit where he's concerned!" She grabbed a towel and dried her hands. "I'm surprised you gave him the time of day, Rob. You know how I feel about him."

Robert's look of discomfort increased. "It's not that I mean to be disloyal or anything like that, Jacqui, but I think you're wrong to refuse to see him."

She looked at his earnest expression, and felt a pang. She and her stepbrother rarely had any kind of disagreement. "You just don't know what it was like for my mother and me after Dad was killed, Rob." She moved to the window and looked out, her expression somber. "All the scandal—the gossip—most of Mother's so-called friends didn't want to know her anymore. They said she might have been partly to blame for what happened to Dad; some even said that she might have plotted with Benjamin to cause the accident. Can you imagine?"

She turned her face toward Robert; tears sparkled in her eyes. "Mother couldn't even kill a moth that flew into the house. I've seen her spend the better part of an hour trying to maneuver one outside without hurting it."

"Anyone who really knew her wouldn't believe the gossip."

The corners of Jacqui's mouth turned down. "But there never would have been any gossip if Benjamin hadn't come into our lives . . . if he hadn't forced Dad to take a job working in his damned mine. Dad hated being underground; he loved the sun, loved to laugh. I can still hear him, sometimes, laughing with my mother, teasing her . . . We were happy, Rob. I know your dad was good to her, after they married. And she did love Anton. But she was never quite the same.

Sometimes she used to go off into a world of her own, and I was afraid she'd never come back to us.''

Robert came up behind her and squeezed her shoulders encouragingly. ''I understand those times were painful for you, Jacqui, but it wasn't only your mother who had to deal with the scandal. You don't believe your uncle deliberately set up that mine accident, do you?''

She sighed and turned to face him. ''I've read the investigator's report a dozen times. According to the evidence, it was Dad himself who set those faulty fuses. But I have good reason to believe Benjamin was morally responsible, if nothing else. He forced my dad to go down in the mine that day, and that was what made Dad so upset he didn't take proper precautions.''

''But that's not the same thing as causing the accident. Everybody makes mistakes, Jacqui. If your uncle made one with your dad, can't you find it in your heart to forgive him?''

''No, the best I can do is to bury the past and get on with my life,'' she replied grimly. ''Something I was doing quite well until Zane Dantine showed up today.''

After a brief pause, Robert observed, ''I used to think you had a crush on Dantine, at least back when you were in high school. I saw you cut his picture out of a magazine once. Some picture of him and Treherne at a Senate hearing—you kept it on your bureau for a while.''

Jacqui moved away abruptly. Her laugh was a little ragged. ''Me? Have a crush on Treherne's hatchet man? If I cut out the picture, it was probably for a school report or something.''

She turned suddenly and threw out her hands. "Look, it's a waste of time talking about the past. Shouldn't we get busy making out the supply lists for the trek schedule? You know how fast the time slips away. And I bet you've left half the meal plans for me to do, haven't you?"

Her long-legged stride carried her to the door leading outside. Robert followed more slowly. But, to her relief, he let the argument drop. Soon they were busy with lists and schedules, and she sought forgetfulness in the comfort of routine tasks. But Jacqui couldn't do much about the dull ache around her heart. Zane Dantine's sudden reappearance in her life had seen to that.

A few miles away in a luxury apartment in the Sun Valley Lodge, Benjamin Treherne, CEO and majority stockholder of one of the world's most powerful mining corporations, looked up at his right-hand man and asked, "Isn't there anything more you can do? I've got to see her soon, or—" The urgency in the old man's voice was painful for Zane to hear.

"I haven't given up yet. There must be some other angle that will break through those walls she's built up against you."

"Be careful with her. Between her folks and me, she's been hurt enough."

"Don't worry. She's stronger than you might think." Zane hesitated, then added, "She has a look sometimes that's you all over. When she sets her chin, she looks the same way you do when you're facing a boardroom full of lawyers."

"Does she?" Benjamin glanced up, a spark in his eye. Then he sighed. "I always thought she looked a great deal like her mother. Leah was very beautiful."

The crease between Zane's brows deepened. "I can't understand why Jacqui still blames you for her father's death. It goes against logic, and she's an intelligent woman."

"Sometimes logic doesn't come into it, lad. But in this case, Jacqui has reason to blame me. I blame myself."

"But the mine explosion was an accident. I checked the facts myself, years ago."

Benjamin cast him a quizzical look. "Did you, now? I should have known you'd check. You don't take anything for granted."

"I had to know Jacqui's side of it, just in case—"

"Just in case the old man really might be a murderer? Well, sit down, lad. I'll tell you what didn't show up in the official account."

Benjamin fumbled in his vest pocket for his pipe; then stared at it for a moment and said, "Don't know why I carry this thing since Doc says I can't smoke it. Oh, well." He put the pipe away, then placed his hands on his knees as if to brace himself.

"The day before my brother, Johnny, died, we had one hell of a quarrel. Among other things, I told him I'd sooner see him dead than watch him go on breaking Leah's heart with his running around. I didn't know Jacqui was sitting with a book in a window seat in that room. I hoped she hadn't understood all I'd said, but she'd heard me tell Johnny to go back into the mine to finish the job he'd started, opening up a new tunnel." Benjamin stopped to draw in a deep breath. "You know what happened. Three men dead,

including Johnny. I went to tell Leah. Jacqui was
there, too. Her face was dead white—eyes like burned
holes in a blanket. God, I've never forgotten the way
she accused me with her eyes.''

He winced and closed his eyes. "She's cut me out of
her life ever since. I thought she'd grow out of it. But
she hasn't. And now time's running out. I need to
square things with her somehow..." His voice trailed
away, then he opened his eyes and with renewed urgency said, "Help me get through to her, Zane. Just
get me the chance to talk with her. It's the most important job I've ever asked you to do. It's the real
reason I called you back from Central America."

"I understand." Zane thought briefly of Jacqui's
angry words and stony expression when he'd seen her
that afternoon. "I'll do my damnedest for you. But
you have to realize I'm not on Jacqui's list of favorite
people myself."

"You'll bring her around, I know you will."

Zane ran his hand around the back of his neck.
Sure, he thought. *But I have a hunch it might be an
easier job negotiating with those rebel miners in Central America.*

Chapter Two

The following morning, after helping Jacqui bring in some of the stock that had been running free in the pasture, Robert apologized for leaving her on her own that day.

"I have to see the man at my bank about my credit line for the coming year," he explained. "I made the appointment last week, or else I wouldn't—"

"That's okay, Rob," Jacqui said with a wave of her hand. "I'd just as soon spend some time getting the horses used to me again. They'll have to know who's boss when we go out on the trail."

After Robert had gone, Jacqui set out the bucket and grooming equipment. She hoped the familiar routine of caring for the horses would help her get a grip on feelings that weren't at all settled.

Everything's different, she thought as she went into the barn. *This summer was supposed to be a change-*

over time—time for myself before I started out on a
new job. Everything was under control. But now...

An image of Zane Dantine flashed into her mind,
scattering her thoughts. Damn! She used the curry
comb so vigorously that the horse she was working on
shifted away in protest. "Sorry, old fellow," she said
aloud in apology, then went on combing with less
force.

Grooming Robert's string of horses was hot, tiring
work. First she had to dip muddy tails into the bucket
of soapy water, then comb out mud and burrs from
tails and manes, then go over every inch of dusty hide
with brushes and clean water. The horses loved it,
whuffling from time to time in response to the one-
sided remarks she made to them, nudging her shoulder as she worked on them. After a couple of hours,
she felt relief from the muscle tension that had accu-
mulated since the day before. She gave the horse she
was grooming a friendly thump with the flat of her
hand when he shied away from entering the stall where
his lunch awaited him. "Go on in, you big baby," she
scolded. "It's only a stack of hay, not a coyote."

After emptying the latest batch of dirty water from
her bucket, she set it under the tap to refill. The water, coming cold from the tap, splashed invitingly. She
cupped her hand under the stream, then splashed
handfuls of the cool liquid over her hot face and
throat. It felt wonderful. She scooped up another
handful to let it trickle down the open throat of her
cotton shirt.

"That's one way to stay cool."

The deep voice from the stable entrance brought her
spinning around. Her foot caught the bucket, and it
toppled over. Water gushed across the hard-packed

earth to within an inch of the boots of the man standing in the doorway. "Zane!" she exclaimed. "What are you doing here?"

He came inside, moving with a predatorlike quietness that set her heart pounding. The tension she'd worked so hard to erase came back in a rush. He looked different. She'd never seen him in anything except business suits, never in ordinary work clothes like he was wearing now. In nondescript jeans, faded checked shirt and scuffed boots, he could have been one of the wranglers who worked on Anton's horse ranch.

The warning bells clamoring in her head reminded her this was no wrangler she had to deal with. She braced herself as he approached her. His penetrating gaze rested on her wet face, then dropped lower to the dripping front of her blouse.

She saw clearly the amusement that flashed briefly in his eyes before he drawled, "I'm glad you're making an effort to stay cool. It'll help us get through our talk with a minimum of stress."

She stiffened. But before she could open her mouth for a hot retort, he took her breath away by reaching out to touch her hair. "Hold still," he said. "Your hair clasp is falling out."

She jerked her head away, and the clasp went flying. Her dark hair came tumbling down around her face and shoulders. "Don't touch me!" Her voice lashed at him. "I told you never to touch me again..." Her voice trailed off as she realized how much she'd given away in her hasty words.

Some emotion flashed in his eyes, but it was quickly doused. He withdrew his hand and said, "If there's one thing I can depend on with you, Jacqui, it's that you never forget. Or forgive."

A shiver passed over her. The barn that had seemed overheated a moment ago now seemed chilly and cramped for space. Or was it just that no space would seem big enough for the disturbance she felt at being this close to the man she thought she'd successfully blocked from her memory?

I've got to get out of here. Without a word, she brushed past him and hurried through the doorway.

A few steps from the barn, she stopped. No, she wouldn't run from him. She moved toward the last horse waiting to be groomed. Her senses, keenly attuned to Zane, heard the faint tread of his footsteps as he followed her. It took an effort of will to smother the feeling of being cornered and to keep her reaction from showing on her face. She turned to look at him as he came to a halt at her side. "All right," she said, "I can see you're not going to give up until you get whatever you're here for off your chest. So let's get it over. What do you want from me?"

"BJ wants to see you. He's staying just a few miles away in Sun Valley, at the Lodge."

She felt a painful tightening in her chest. "The answer is no. Anything else?"

He made no effort to conceal his displeasure as he looked at her set expression. "I know how you feel about your uncle. You're mistaken, and I probably can't do much about that. But I'm here to tell you that you *are* going to see him—today, if possible. And you're going to act civil to him. You owe him that much, and I'm here to see that you pay up."

"What are you talking about? I don't owe Benjamin Treherne a thing."

"You owe him plenty."

She felt heat rise in her body. "What I owe him, he can be glad I'm not repaying. Believe me, Zane, you're doing him no favor trying to get us together. So for the last time, just drop it."

He stepped closer to her, his eyes flashing cold fire. "Not this time, Jacqui. There's something you don't know. BJ is ill—seriously ill. He needs some contact with the last living member of his family. Don't you think he's suffered enough for what happened nearly twenty years ago? He lost a brother—"

"And I lost a father! If Benjamin is trying to appease his conscience at this late date, he shouldn't expect me to make it easy for him. Because I can't and won't."

"God, you can be hard sometimes." Zane's gaze swept over her rigid form, lingered on the straight line of her mouth, then returned to meet her defiant gaze. "You're really something to look at, Jacqui. You've got what it takes to stop a man in his tracks and make him look, then look again. But inside you, where it counts—"

She braced herself for what he'd say next. His eyes narrowed, seemed to look inside her. Without moving, she felt as though he'd come breathtakingly close. In spite of herself, her breathing quickened, and her fingers clenched tightly against her palms.

"Inside you, Jacqui," he went on, "you've put up walls, locked away your compassion. BJ is sick, he's old and he feels he needs your forgiveness."

Zane's gaze locked on hers, compelling her, willing her to relent, to give Benjamin what he wanted. *Just like last time,* she thought, and felt the tightness around her rib cage increase. *That's what he's paid to do, after all.*

"I used to think Benjamin was a clever man," she said finally. "He couldn't be so smart if he picked you to be his messenger. Does he think I'd forget what happened the last time he sent you? Or didn't you tell him about the method you used to get him what he wanted then?"

Once again she saw that flicker of raw emotion in his eyes. A muscle jumped in his jaw. "Jacqui—you've got it all twisted. I never meant to hurt you."

"No, of course not." She used irony to keep her anger in check. "You had a job to do, and you did it. I made an easy target, didn't I? Young and foolish enough to believe that you really cared for me."

His mouth taut, Zane said, "I did care. You'd been at the hospital at least thirty hours without a break, watching over your mother. I took you out of there because you needed food and rest."

Her eyes darkened and she stepped closer to him. "But I didn't need the phony love scene. That was a trick to keep me out of the way while Benjamin Treherne wormed his way in to see my mother."

"There was nothing phony about what happened between us—then or any other time. I tried to talk to you later, but you wouldn't let me near you, remember?"

"The last thing I needed was more of your smooth excuses. And there's no point in talking about it now. I just don't have time for this."

She turned and groped for the tie reins of the remaining horse waiting for his turn to be groomed. Zane reached out to stop her, but she dodged and vaulted to the horse's bare back. The horse shied, and she felt the tremor of powerful muscles between her thighs; he hadn't been ridden yet this spring, and wasn't sure he liked the idea. She tightened her leg muscles, and the horse steadied.

She saw Zane move to block her path. Eyes blazing in her pale face, she looked down at him. "Get out of my way, Zane. I have to exercise this horse."

"Don't be so foolish as to ride him without a saddle. He's so keyed up he'll dump you within a mile."

"It's nothing to do with you one way or the other, Zane Dantine. Now, move!" She touched her heels to the gelding's sides and started off in a flurry. Zane called after her, but the sound of hoofbeats in her ears drowned out his words. She bent her efforts to curbing her mount's attempts to take charge of the light halter, which was all that gave her a measure of control.

She didn't really see the trail as it flashed by; her thoughts were back in that hospital room six years before. Herself, flushed and glowing from the wonder of those magic moments with Zane; and then...

The wonder had evaporated the instant she'd seen Benjamin Treherne seated at her mother's bedside, holding her hand, his shoulders slumped and his head bowed. Her mother's face was pale but peaceful, and with tearing grief, Jacqui knew that the struggle was over at last.

Everything after that was a haze. Anton came in and Benjamin left, his face twisted and old looking. She hadn't seen Zane again until the funeral. By then she'd figured out why he'd come, why he'd taken her away from her mother's bedside. He'd diverted her attention so that Benjamin could steal the last moments of her mother's life. Not only from Anton, but from her, Jacqui. To the pain of losing her mother was added the pain of Zane's betrayal.

It was then the delicate tendrils of her newfound feelings for him had curled up and died. When he'd tried to speak with her after the funeral, she'd turned on him with words that scorched and burned, determined to protect herself from further pain. He'd tried to take her in his arms, and it was then that she'd screamed for him never to touch her again.

Robert had intervened and led her away, sobbing. She'd refused to see Zane in person in the six years since that day. At her insistence, lawyers had handled the details of her father's trust fund.

The gelding stumbled, pulling her thoughts back into the present. Briefly she regretted the lack of a proper bridle and bit. But she'd learned to ride with nothing more than a clump of mane clutched in her fists, so now she hung on, her jaw clamped in determination.

They reached the fork that led upward to the foothills behind the cabin; the gelding slowed on the rougher trail. Her ears picked up the sounds from the trail behind. Another horse was coming up fast. A glance over her shoulder told her it was Zane, also riding bareback, on the black horse that had been in the first stall inside the barn. Jacqui urged the gelding onto a shortcut, a rock gully that led steeply upward. The gelding snorted in protest as his hooves scrambled for footing, but he obeyed, lunging forward and almost unseating her. She heard Zane call out behind her and spared him another quick glance.

He was catching up with her. She saw his face, grimly set as he kept an iron grip on the reins. Unlike her, Zane had taken time to put a proper bridle and bit on his mount. But it still called for skill she hadn't known he possessed, for him to control the black without a saddle. She saw the muscles straining against the fabric of his clothes as he kept control mainly with his body, just as she was. His hair, thick and dark and unruly, caught glints of light from the sun. Her throat went dry. The compelling attraction she'd always had toward him surged within her. She fought to ignore it and failed. *Oh, God—is it going to happen to me again?*

After a final tricky scramble, she reached the top. The foothill's crest overlooked a spectacular view of the valley. Jacqui headed for a twisted sycamore, slipped from the horse's back, then tossed the reins over a low branch.

Ignoring Zane, who'd topped the rise only seconds after her, she looked out over the view while he dismounted. She didn't acknowledge his presence when he came to stand beside her. Inside, the tug-of-war in her feelings about him continued.

"Jacqui, listen to me." His voice was urgent. "What happened between us that day at the hospital had nothing to do with Benjamin or anything else. I didn't start out to make love to you—I only wanted to take care of you, to comfort you, I swear it."

Still breathing rapidly from the rough ride, she refused to look at him, trying to deny the unwanted tumult he created in her.

"No, look at me." Zane took her by the shoulders and made her face him. His gaze compelled her to listen. "When I kissed you that first time, it was innocent. You were hurting—I didn't know how else to tell you how much I hurt for you. Then things changed.

You kissed me back. God help me, I wouldn't have been human not to go on kissing you."

"You took advantage of me. You were older, I was vulnerable."

He winced at her accusing cry, but his grip tightened, preventing her from pulling away. "Okay, I admit it was wrong, but I couldn't believe the change in you when you kissed me back. I'd been forcing myself to think of you as a teenager, out-of-bounds, not to be touched. Then there you were in my arms, all woman, more passionate than I'd dreamed—"

She twisted away from him and covered her eyes. "Oh, God, don't remind me; I was so ashamed afterward."

"Ashamed? But why?"

She faced him again, head high, her eyes tormented. "I was making love with you while my mother was dying!"

"Jacqui, have you been blaming yourself for that all this time? Is that why you refused to see or talk to me again?"

Ignoring the urgency in his voice, she wrapped her arms around herself and stared blindly out over the valley. "I couldn't bear to be reminded; I didn't even want to think about those hours I spent with you that day."

He expelled a deep breath. This time she offered no resistance when he reached for her and pulled her gently to him. His hand touched her hair, stroking the tangled strands with infinite care, as though afraid she'd bolt at any moment. "Don't punish yourself for being human, Jacqui. The mind has to protect itself from too much grief. You let yourself go with me because it was a way to forget for a little while."

The simplicity of his words and the conviction in his voice penetrated the barriers she'd erected against the old guilt. For a moment, she allowed herself to relax against him, let herself absorb his warmth, his manly scent, his strength. It was an effort to push herself away, out of his arms. "What you say may be partly true, Zane. God knows I'd like to believe there was some excuse for the way I behaved."

She raised a shaking hand and pushed the hair back from her eyes. With painful honesty she went on, "But whatever face I put on it, it's a fact that for a while, there in that car with you, I forgot all about Mother, and everything else. I only thought about you and how you made me feel."

"And how do you feel about me now?"

Time stilled. She was intensely aware not only of the man facing her but of the faint pulse of life on the breeze-swept hilltop. The scent of sweet new grass, crushed beneath their feet, came to her with every uneven breath she took; the raucous cry of a hawk from somewhere in the distance was a counterpoint to the thudding pace of her own heartbeat. "Tell me the truth, Zane," she asked at last. "Did you take me away from the hospital to keep me occupied while Benjamin saw my mother?"

He hesitated just long enough for the tiny hope inside her to flicker and die. "I can't say that wasn't part of it. Everyone knew you would have thrown a major fit if he'd tried to see her while you were there."

"I see." Disappointment was bitter in her mouth as she fixed her gaze on the distant rooftops of Ketchum and Sun Valley.

He wasn't through. "But the main reason I took you out of there was just as I said: you needed the break."

"And incidentally giving Benjamin his chance to sneak in," she retorted.

"Haven't you ever wondered how Benjamin knew to come to the hospital that day?"

She turned her head to stare at him. "What are you saying?"

"I'm saying that it was your mother who asked to see Benjamin. She had Anton call and ask him to come."

Shock held Jacqui still. "I don't believe you. Benjamin was—Anton wouldn't—"

"Benjamin meant more to your mother than you ever wanted to believe. Anton knew that, if you didn't. He was prepared to be more generous."

"But she hated Benjamin. He was her enemy. He—"

Zane took her by the shoulders. His eyes flared with some emotion other than anger. "How long are you going to keep the blinders on, Jacqui? You're a woman now. Where's your mercy, your compassion?"

"What do you care? What difference can it make to you?" The question was torn from her. In spite of herself, his closeness made her breathing quicken and her pulse leap.

"Because I blame myself for making things worse for you when you were already so upset about your mother. I hated hurting you, even though I didn't intend to. I don't want to hurt you now."

"You don't have to worry. I'm a lot tougher than I was back then. You couldn't hurt me now."

"Can't I?" His voice was rough. "I'm glad to hear it. I'm glad you're not twenty anymore, or a vulnerable teenager. I've wondered what it would be like to meet you again on equal terms. I've wondered if the fire would still be there if I did...this." His hands slid from her shoulders up to cradle her head.

And then her thoughts and angry protest splintered into a thousand shards of sensation as he kissed her. Feelings she'd tried to bury years ago thrust upward within her like wildwood growth in springtime, famished for life-giving water. Spears of fire found targets in her most secret places; hunger leaped into life. Mechanically she tried to push him away, but too much of her wanted him to stay, for the kiss to go on. Instead of pushing, her hands slid around his waist and clung tightly to his belt. The sounds of their uneven breathing blurred with other small sounds on the hilltop: the rustle of the breeze through nearby brush, the faint crack of a twig as Zane moved his feet to brace his legs more firmly, to hold her more closely to him.

When at last he lifted his head, she stared up at him, amazed at this resurrection of her passionate feelings for him. His eyes looked dark and turbulent as he stared back at her. For a moment, with their heartbeats separated only by a few centimeters of flesh and cotton, she felt a yearning so strong it terrified her. She pulled away, eluding him when he would have reached for her again.

"You shouldn't have done that." Her voice was too high, scarcely sounding like her own.

He watched her with narrowed, intent eyes. "Why not? The fire *is* still there—you can't deny it. We can start over again, Jacqui, wipe out the past—"

"Can we? You're still Benjamin Treherne's man, aren't you? You're only here now because he wants something from me."

He stared at her, his brow darkening. "Dammit, Jacqui, what BJ wants doesn't have anything to do with us."

She rose swiftly and went over to the gelding. As she snatched up the reins, she said, "That's what you said six years ago. You'd better stay away from me, Zane. You're nothing but trouble as far as I'm concerned."

"Jacqui, don't go. This isn't settled yet."

She grabbed a handful of mane and vaulted onto the horse. "What's there to settle? You have your loyalties and I have mine."

He started to lay his hand on hers, and she pulled back, causing the gelding to dance away a few steps. "You said before that I wasn't one to forgive and forget easily, but you're wrong. I do want to forget. I want to look ahead, not back. Goodbye, Zane."

Wheeling the gelding, she touched her heels to his side and plunged off the hilltop onto the trail back to the cabin. True to her word, she didn't look back.

In the luxurious private suite at Sun Valley Lodge, Benjamin Treherne was silent for a long time after he'd heard Zane's report. Then he sighed heavily. "Do you think I'm wrong, to keep on trying to reach her?"

Zane walked over to gaze out the window at the spacious green lawns below. Moodily he replied, "She's closed her mind. It may be impossible to reach her."

"It's funny how things turn out," Benjamin mused. "When Johnny and I were kids, he was always trying to beat me in whatever game we were playing. He hardly ever won, because he was younger and smaller. But he used to laugh and swear that someday he'd come in first and leave me in the dust. It seems now he was right."

Zane turned abruptly from the window. "I don't see what else we can do about the situation, short of kidnapping her." He grimaced at his own irony.

Benjamin sighed. "She's like the wild creatures she loves so much. She's been burned, and now she's too skittish to trust any of us."

"You're right about that." There was an edge to Zane's voice.

Benjamin looked at him sharply, then said, "There is one more thing we might try. It's not exactly kidnapping, but with a little finesse, we might be able to pull it off."

"What are you talking about?"

With his fingers tented under his chin, Benjamin looked off into space and said, "I've talked to Robert Janek. I think he might be reasonable about booking us on one of his treks. With six or seven days together on the trail, I think maybe there'd be a chance to convince Jacqui that I'm not quite the shark she thinks I am."

Zane stared at him, then exclaimed, "That's crazy. Not only don't I see a hope in hell that Jacqui would agree to go, but you simply couldn't take a trip like that. Your heart—"

"What about my heart? The doc said as long as I keep taking my medicine I can handle a fair amount of exercise. He said it'd even be good for me."

"He wasn't talking about your going on some fool trip into the mountains!"

Benjamin slammed the palm of his hand down on the arm of his chair. "Dammit, Zane, I'm tired of sitting around waiting to die, puttering with a bit of fishing, a round or two of golf. If I have to go, I'd just as soon it was on a horse in the mountains. The Sawtooths are special, lad. I spent a lot of time up there, twenty years ago. I wouldn't mind seeing them again."

Zane hunkered down on his heels in front of Benjamin, bringing his eyes on level with the tired eyes looking back at him. Urgently he said, "Don't do this, BJ. It could all be for nothing. Your niece is a very stubborn woman."

The old man smiled. "No, Zane, I think we'll have to give this a try, if Janek will cooperate. Before, I've always sent you to talk to Jacqui because I thought a personal visit from me would do more harm than good. Now I don't think I have that much to lose. If this fails, I'll give it up—let her go her own way without any more interference from me. Tell her that. It might be the right incentive." His mouth twisted wryly.

"It'll never work."

"Zane, it isn't just for me, not anymore. I need to square things before I cash in my chips, true. But it's clear to me now that Jacqui needs to square things in her own mind even more. I was wrong to put it off for so long."

"But, dammit, BJ—"

"Now don't argue, Zane. Just help me get through this with the least amount of damage possible. If things don't work out—well, I'll have tried. Will you help me?"

Zane got to his feet. Throwing up his hands in resignation, he said, "You know I will. God knows I always have before."

"Good lad. You won't be sorry. Get Janek on the phone, will you?"

Chapter Three

Robert, no!'' Jacqui's voice rang out across the corral. "I can't believe you'd agree to that!"

Robert awkwardly twisted the bridle he held in his hands. "Jacqui, if you'd only listen—"

"Listen to what? Listen to how Benjamin Treherne talked you into the craziest idea I've ever heard? Take him on a trek up into the Sawtooths? There's no way I'll go along with that scheme." She began to pace up and down, her body taut.

"It's only a short trek," Robert repeated doggedly. "It has to be an easy one, on account of his health. And you don't have to go if you don't want to. I can take one of Dad's wranglers, instead. I made sure Treherne understood it was up to you whether you went along or not."

She stopped pacing and planted her fists on her hips. "Was this trek Benjamin's idea or Zane's?"

"How should I know?" Robert threw up his hands. "Okay, I know I should have consulted with you before taking on the job. But I knew you'd make a fuss."

"Then why did you say yes?"

"Because I thought it was time you stopped running away."

Her eyes widened in disbelief. "Me, run away? What are you talking about?"

Robert smacked the bridle against his leg. "I'm talking about the fact that for years you've acted like Benjamin was some sort of bogeyman, the worst monster to come along since Dracula. Well, he's no Dracula; he's just a man. An old and sick man. He wants to see you and talk to you, and he's willing to agree to anything you want just for the chance."

"If he's so sick, he shouldn't be going up in the mountains anyway," she asserted.

"He said he had clearance from his doctor. Besides, you know we can't get into the really tough trails until more of the snow melts higher up."

"I don't like it," she said shortly. "He's plotting something."

"For Pete's sake!"

"Apparently he's sold you on the idea. But I'm not buying. You know how he——"

"Jacqui, I get so tired of hearing that old story. Personally I think there could be another side to it. You always claimed he was your mother's enemy. But I never heard her say that."

"What do you mean? I saw her burn some letters he sent her, without reading them first. She'd walk out of the room if his name was mentioned. That gossip about them having an affair—surely you don't believe that was true."

"No, of course not. All I'm trying to say is that you don't really know what was in your mother's mind. Maybe all she wanted was to live down the gossip. Maybe she didn't blame him as much as you did."

Jacqui stared at him, biting her lip. She hated arguing with Robert like this. But how could she tell him that while he was certain the rumors about her mother's involvement with Benjamin hadn't been true, she herself wasn't so sure? Reluctantly she asked, "Rob, Zane said something about Mother asking to see Benjamin before she died. Do you know if that was true?"

Robert hesitated, then replied, "Yes, it is. Dad told me she asked him to send for Benjamin. He flew in on his company plane that same day."

She blinked rapidly, feeling as though the ground beneath her feet was changing into shifting sand. "Why didn't anyone tell me?"

"Nobody could tell you anything, then. If Benjamin's name was so much as mentioned, you'd fly higher than a kite."

"There was nothing she could have wanted to say to him," Jacqui insisted, arguing with herself as much as Robert. "He did too much to hurt her."

"Whatever reason she had to hate him, she must have forgiven him, Jacqui. Dad said her last hours were peaceful."

Jacqui made a gesture of dismissal, but Robert went on inexorably. "If she could forgive him, Jacqui, why can't you?"

Another voice spoke from behind her. "Yes, Jacqui. Why can't you?"

She spun around. Absorbed in her confrontation with Robert, she hadn't heard Zane's car arrive, or his footsteps when he'd come up to the corral fence. Now he stood with one boot propped up on the lower rail, looking at her over the top. She let her anger and confusion overflow onto this new target.

"This trek was your idea, wasn't it? You couldn't get me to agree to see your boss, so you went behind my back and got Rob involved."

Robert made a protesting movement, then something unspoken passed between the two men and he muttered something and hurried away toward the barn. Facing Zane alone, Jacqui declared, "You can get one thing straight, Zane. Robert can do what he wants to—it's his guide service. But I won't be going with you." She started to turn away.

"Wait—you say you want BJ to leave you alone. If you'll give him this one week, he says he'll never bother you again."

His words stopped her. Wariness narrowed her eyes as she wheeled to look at him again. "He said that?"

"Yes. And you can be sure he'll keep his word."

She considered this for a moment, then shook her head. "I don't see the point, Zane. Spending a week on the trail with him wouldn't change anything."

Zane's expression scarcely altered, but she caught a flash of steel in his gray eyes. "Then you leave me no alternative but to give you a stronger reason to change your mind."

Her shoulders tensed as her wariness increased. "What are you talking about?"

"You're in BJ's debt more than you know."

"You've said that before. I don't owe him a thing."

"No? Your education alone cost thousands."

"My father's trust fund covered that. Also any administration fees due to Benjamin as Dad's executor. The lawyers showed me—"

"You saw the papers that spelled out the trust fund terms, signed by your father. What you didn't see were the securities that financed the trust."

"So?"

"So they were worth about half their face value. It was Benjamin who made up the initial difference. Plus he personally put a lot of time and trouble into making them grow and produce the income you needed. He worked as hard on that measly trust fund as he did on any of his own business affairs."

"I don't believe it. Why would he do that?"

"Because he cared about you, and he knew damned well you and your mother wouldn't take a dime from him otherwise."

She shook her head. "I may believe many things, Zane, but never that he cared anything about us. If he did what you say, he must have had some other motive."

Zane's mouth turned down as he looked at her. "You're not going to give an inch, are you? Well, whatever you believe about his motives, it's a fact that without Benjamin's help, you would have had to scrape for your education. You might not have had such a happy home all those years, either. The bank that gave Anton Janek the loan he needed to start his horse ranch did so with private backing from Benjamin."

The uncompromising look in Zane's eyes told her that she could check the facts if she wanted to. Her anger dissipated in a wave of dread. Why would her uncle do all the things Zane said he'd done? What other facts would she discover if she dug deep enough? Instinctively she took a step back and straightened her shoulders to keep Zane from seeing the effect his

words had on her. "All right, you've made your case.
I'll think about it. But I still can't promise I'll do what
you want. I don't like being blackmailed."

She'd spoken quietly, but knew her words had stung
him. His jaw tightened before he said, "I hoped it
wouldn't come to this. If you'd been reasonable—"

"Come off it, Zane. I'm only surprised Benjamin
hasn't called in this debt before now."

"If it was up to BJ, you'd never have known about
the money," Zane retorted. "He doesn't know I'm
telling you now. Personally I think it's time you
learned how much he's done for you."

"I see." Pride kept her head high. Turning, she put
her fingers to her lips and emitted a high, piercing
whistle. From somewhere on the property, a dog's
bark answered her. To Zane, she said in a brittle voice,
"You're right, of course. I should have been told. I
should even thank you for telling me. But frankly, I
don't feel very grateful. I feel sick."

Buddy ran up to them, panting. She bent over the
dog, burying her fingers in the thick fur of his ruff. In
a muffled voice, she said, "I have to go into town now.
I'll let you know later what I've decided about the
trek."

She avoided his gaze as she swung herself up and
over the corral fence. Buddy took a running jump and
scrambled over behind her. She walked in the direction of her car, swerving neither right nor left.

It was a short drive to town, but she didn't go all the
way into Ketchum. Instead she took the road that
branched off to Sun Valley. In a few moments, she
turned into the curving driveway that led up to the
main entrance of the Lodge. But the same blind in-

stinct that had brought her there suddenly faltered, and she pulled over to the side and stopped. *Now why did I come here?* she asked herself as she stared at the buildings up ahead.

Sun Valley Lodge was the kind of place a man like Benjamin Treherne would choose to stay in. Built more than fifty years before as a rustic ski resort patterned after the great ski centers of Switzerland and Austria, the lodge had long ago established itself as one of the world's premier playgrounds. Benjamin was just one more in a long parade of the wealthy, the powerful and the merely famous who traveled from around the world to enjoy the lodge's amenities.

Her hands tightened on the steering wheel. *Mother, you must have known about those securities. Why did you let him do it? Was it true what they said about you and Benjamin?*

For a moment, she allowed herself to think about the doubts she'd buried so deeply. But she couldn't cope with the feelings of disloyalty toward her gentle mother. *It can't be true,* she thought in a brief flash of anguish. *I won't believe it's true.* Her thoughts sought another outlet for her emotions and found one. Zane was her real adversary in all this. He'd blackmailed her—held her debt over her head—all just to satisfy his boss's whim. Her fingers on the steering wheel whitened at the knuckles.

It's got to stop, she told herself, and knew why she'd come to Sun Valley. She had to face Benjamin, tell him that she'd pay him back somehow for what he'd put into her trust fund, but that she couldn't go on that trek. Straightening, she put the Chevy into gear again and drove on to the lodge. A few minutes later, she entered the main lobby. "Benjamin Treherne—where is he staying?" she asked the clerk.

The clerk offered to ring Benjamin's suite for her, but there was no answer. About to turn away, she was stopped by a man she vaguely recognized as a local fisherman who worked as a guide during the summer season.

"You're Robert Janek's sister, aren't you? Don't you work with him sometimes?"

"That's right."

"I heard you asking for Benjamin Treherne. I just left him on Steven's Creek, fishing."

"Really? That's odd—I heard he wasn't well."

"Him, sick?" The guide laughed. "Seemed healthy enough to me. He cussed me out good and proper for trying to help him net a trout, then sent me back here to get me out from underfoot."

"Where exactly on Steven's Creek did you leave him?"

A few minutes later, she was back on the road that led out of town, heading for the spot described by the guide. After parking the car on the roadside, she and Buddy made their way toward the stream, which they could hear gurgling through the brush and trees.

When she first saw him, all she could think of was that Zane's picture of him as being seriously ill was totally wrong. There was Benjamin, wearing high-top waders, standing crouched over in the middle of the stream, arms extended, his eyes following the movement at the end of his line with intense concentration.

"Come on, you finny little devil, admit you're beat!"

She heard the excitement in his voice, the determination; his white hair was ruffled, sticking out in all directions. From this angle, she couldn't see his face, but guessed that it was alight with the urge for conquest. No doubt he went after everything with that same acquisitive fervor—even a harmless trout wasn't exempt.

What do I think I can accomplish by facing him down? she asked herself. *The money he spent on me must seem like pennies to him. He's not going to be put off until he gets whatever it is he wants from me.*

Her intention to confront Benjamin dissipated. Her mouth felt dry; she had the sense of fate closing in on her, and she wasn't ready. As soundlessly as she'd come, she retreated, with Buddy close at her heels. She put five miles of hard driving on the car, her face bleak, before Buddy's whine recalled her attention.

"Sorry, Buddy, old boy." She slowed the car and gave her companion a quick glance of apology. "This isn't going to solve anything, is it? Let's go home—I have some heavy thinking to do."

Jacqui's room at the cabin was on the opposite end from Robert's. Used during the rest of the year as a spare bedroom and catchall room, it still bore the unmistakable traces of her seasonal occupancy. A row of boots were lined up on the closet floor; her all-weather gear hung on a hook. A colorful woven blanket in reds and browns, which she'd picked up in Santa Fe once on a field trip, was spread over the bed. The child-size but real bow-and-arrow set her grandfather had made for her twenty years before hung on a nail over the bed. Other trophies adorned the walls: an eagle's feather, prize ribbons from the three years she'd spent riding in horse shows and a framed chalk portrait she'd made of her grandfather the year she took an art class in high school.

She walked over to stand before the portrait, her face troubled. Aloud she said softly, "Gramps, I wish you were here to help me with this."

Calm, wise eyes looked back at her from the wall. Although the sketch wasn't a perfect likeness of Jim Littlewolf, she'd captured some of the unquenchable spirit and self-reliance that went with his chosen way of life. He was wearing the deerskin leggings and tunic he'd made himself. She'd drawn him sitting on the porch of his mountain cabin, his fingers busy with a piece of leather work, looking straight at her with a half smile on his face.

She felt an upwelling of love for him, and sorrow that he no longer roamed his beloved wilderness; he'd died only two years before.

"I miss you, Gramps," she whispered. "You always made things seem so simple. But they're not simple—at least, not for me."

She heard a door slam. "Jacqui? Are you back?" Robert's call was quickly followed by his appearance at her door. He stopped there, his eyes troubled.

She smiled at him. "Come on in, Rob. I'm not going to bite you. I'm sorry I lost my temper with you earlier."

Robert looked relieved as he walked toward her. "I came to tell you I'm sorry I booked that trek without talking to you first. I had no right to interfere. I'll call Dantine and tell him it's all off."

"No, don't do that. I'm still thinking about what's the best thing to do." Her eyes went back to the portrait. "I was just wishing Gramps were here to help me make up my mind."

"You know he'd never do that. He always said we had to stand on our own two feet. Remember that first night he left us to camp out on our own in the woods?"

She smiled again, ruefully. "What I mainly remember was being so scared we spent half the night on the lookout for bears and mountain lions."

"We learned what he wanted us to learn, though. That you have to face up to your fears and conquer them."

"I know what you're getting at, Rob. But you're wrong. I may have been avoiding contact with Benjamin, but that was by choice—I'm not afraid of him."

"Are you sure? There are different kinds of fear."

"What I am afraid of is what might happen if Benjamin and I do spend much time together. It took me a long time to bury the past. Now if he's going to insist on digging it up—"

Robert folded his arms across his chest. His eyes were shrewd as he said, "Maybe it's the idea of having Zane around that bothers you the most."

Her back stiffened. "What's that supposed to mean?"

"I could practically feel the sparks going off between you two this morning. My guess is it wasn't all just anger. I've never seen anybody else get to you that way—not the local fellows or the men who come on the treks. I think you might have cared a lot more about Dantine than you ever let on."

About to hotly deny his charge, she stopped herself, realizing denials were useless. He knew her too well. She jammed her hands into her pockets and said, "Nothing's going to come of it, so it doesn't matter."

"Doesn't it? If he really bothers you, I can understand it would make the trek with Treherne all that
much harder for you. Dantine is a tough man, a loner.
I wouldn't like to see you get seriously mixed up with
him."

"There's no danger in my getting mixed up with
him, I can promise you." Conviction rang in her voice.

"If that's true, then why not go ahead and make the
trek? Give Treherne what he wants—a week of your
time, on your own ground. Then it'll be over and done
with. Treherne and Dantine will go their way, and you
can go yours."

She met Robert's serious look with a grimace of
frustration. "Damn, I wish I hadn't spent all that
money on my education. I'd sooner have waited ta-
bles, scrubbed floors, anything except—" She broke
off, then said, "I suppose I'll have to do it. I don't
want them getting the same idea you had, that I might
be afraid of them."

"Jacqui, you know I'm on your side in all this,
don't you? I don't want you to think I—"

"That's okay, Rob. I understand." She cast a glance
at the portrait on the wall. "I wanted Gramps's ad-
vice, and I think you did a pretty good job of standing in for him." She gave him a hug. "Now get out of
here, will you? I have to figure out what I'm going to
say to Zane that won't make him think I'm giving in
to blackmail."

Half an hour later, after sitting and staring at the
phone for most of that time, she stood up in sudden
decision. *I'd rather tell him to his face,* she thought.
*I'll make sure there's no mistake about the terms. One
week, and that's it.*

She grabbed her windbreaker and left the cabin. Outside she felt the snow-chilled breeze blowing down from the high mountain passes and quickly shrugged into the jacket before climbing into her car. But the down-filled garment didn't do much to relieve the icy knot in her stomach.

Zane slipped his reading glasses off and laid them down on the papers strewed across the desk in front of him. He'd just reached his hand up to his neck to rub away the tension from the past hour's intense concentration when the phone on the desk sounded.

"Dantine here," he said. He listened silently for a moment, then said, "No, I can't come down to the lobby right now. I'm expecting an overseas call on this line. Why not come up here instead?" Another pause, then with a slight edge to his voice, "Yes, I'm alone. You won't run into BJ, if that's what you're worried about."

The receiver hummed the disconnect signal, and he stared at it for a moment before putting it down again. He felt a swift rush of anticipation that quickly faded. Whatever Jacqui had come to say to him probably wouldn't be much to his liking. *She hates my guts for telling her about the money,* he thought. His mouth twisted wryly. *It seems as if I'm always cast in the role of the heavy where she's concerned.*

The phone rang at the same time as the door buzzer. "Hang on a minute while I take this call," he said, waving Jacqui inside. "I won't be long." He strode back to the phone and watched her out of the corner of his eye as he spoke to his caller. "Yes, I got the papers today. Those production figures are way below normal for Costa Rica. One minor political skirmish shouldn't make that much difference. Did you get hold of Morales?''

A part of his mind was detached from the voice that responded to his questions. He saw that Jacqui was too restless to stay in one place. With her hands thrust into the pockets of her windbreaker, she moved restlessly around the room, pausing to look out the window, examining the flowers arranged on a table there. He noted that she gave a wide berth to the smaller portion of the L-shaped room that contained the king-size bed.

The voice in his ear demanded attention. He frowned and replied, ''Yes, that should do it. Get back to me in the morning after you've talked to Morales. I won't be available for several days after that. There aren't any phones where BJ and I are going.''

Overhearing the casual reference to the coming trek, and extremely aware of Zane's appraising stare at her, Jacqui felt a flush mounting to her cheeks. This meeting wasn't starting off the way she'd planned. He was supposed to have answered her summons to meet her in the lobby; she didn't want to have to deal with him in his own territory, especially with that damn bed lurking in the corner. She stood still, watching him as he concluded his call.

He was wearing a dress shirt, open at the collar, and slacks that covered the muscular length of his legs with tailored perfection. The semidressy look somehow suited his rugged features. No one would call him handsome, exactly, but ... She forced her gaze away and saw the glasses lying on the papers on the desk. She was surprised; she hadn't known he wore glasses. *How many other things don't I know about him?* she wondered.

Her hands tightened in the windbreaker's pockets.
Who was Zane, really? In wrangler's clothes, he'd
looked as if he was completely at home on horseback;
he'd ridden well enough to win money in a rodeo. Now
he seemed just as much at home conducting a compli-
cated business negotiation over the telephone.

During the years of her teenage crush on him, she'd
scarcely given a thought to wondering about who and
what he was. At the time, surprisingly, his connection
to her enemy hadn't bothered her so much. Zane had
been so exciting—his work as a troubleshooter in far-
off, glamorous places was fascinating. What with his
interest in her, his questions about her likes and dis-
likes in school, it was no wonder she'd pinned all her
budding young dreams on him, eagerly looking forward to his visits. Back then Benjamin had just been
an ogre in a distant land to her. Zane was the white
knight . . . no, the black knight. So much more exciting . . .

"Would you like a drink?"

She started, called back into the present. He'd
completed his call and now moved toward a cabinet
that bore a decanter and glasses.

"No, thanks." She hesitated, thrown off stride by
his casual manner. He didn't seem in any hurry to
know why she'd come. Abruptly she said, "I came to
tell you I've agreed to take part in the trek Robert
booked for your boss."

He poured a small amount of whiskey into a glass,
then gave her an enigmatic look. "I'm glad to hear it.
BJ will be pleased, too."

Her lips tightened. Apparently he hadn't been worried about what her decision would be, either. "We'll
need a day to finish organizing everything. It's best if

you come to the cabin early on Wednesday—we like to get started by seven o'clock on the first day, if possible. Be sure to bring something warm to wear. This time of year it's hot during the day, but it can get very cold at night.''

He raised his glass to his lips and drank, but his gaze never left her face. ''You could have phoned to tell me all that. Why didn't you?''

In spite of her efforts to prevent it, heat came into her cheeks. ''Because I really came to tell you something else.''

''I see. Well, go on and tell me.''

''I'll do the trek, but I want to confirm that that will be the end of it. No more interference from Benjamin in my life from now on. One week should be enough to convince you both that he's wasting his time with me. Is that agreed?''

Zane nodded. ''Yes. If you still feel the same way when the trek is over.''

''Now, about the money I owe him.''

A frown creased Zane's forehead. ''He doesn't want it back, if that's what you're about to say.''

She ignored the interruption. ''The bank loan to my stepfather was a plain business deal, and whoever backed it made a good investment. Anton is perfectly capable of paying off his own mortgage. But I intend to pay back every cent of what Benjamin put into the trust fund. Not right away, but soon. If you'll just see to it that I have an accurate accounting—''

Zane made a sudden move, and she had to stiffen herself to keep from flinching. For a second, his eyes blazed dangerously. ''You would pay him back, wouldn't you? To the penny. You don't care that—'' He broke off in disgust. ''Oh, hell, have it your way.

I'll see you get the accounting. Just don't mention it to BJ."

Her lip curled. "I plan to have as little to say to him as I can decently manage. As far as I'm concerned, he's just another tourist who wants to see the mountains. At the end of the week, the charade will be at an end. Is that clear?"

"Very clear."

"Then that finishes everything I came to say. I'll see you Wednesday morning."

She got as far as the door before he stopped her. His hand reached the doorknob before hers did. She froze, looking down the length of his arm, so close his sleeve brushed her shoulder. His scent and warmth seemed to encompass her. She glanced up and was caught as though in a net by the gleam of determination in his eyes. He said, "There's one thing you've left out, Jacqui. When this thing with BJ is out of the way, you and I have some unfinished business."

She ignored the hammering of her heart and tilted her chin another degree. "There's nothing unfinished between you and me except saying goodbye, permanently. And that will happen exactly one week from tomorrow. You can count on it."

His eyes held hers, and in the gray depths she imagined she saw the faint flicker of fire. "No, Jacqui—it's not over between us. It's just the beginning."

Chapter Four

Jacqui rose early on Wednesday morning. When she stepped outside the cabin, she walked into a world of misty silence; the sun's rays had not yet had a chance to burn off the dew hazing the grassy fields outside the corral. She looked toward Sun Valley's Mount Baldy and saw the blue sparkle of snow high at the summit.

No chance of the trek being called off, she thought. *It's a perfect day to go up into the Sawtooths. If only Buddy and I were going off on our own, or with Robert...* She sighed and relinquished the tempting thought. She'd made a bargain, and now she was stuck with it.

The routine care of the animals in the barn helped her tamp down the tension, mounting again after a day's respite preparing for the trek. Now there were only a few details to take care of before Zane and Benjamin arrived.

She was pitching hay in the barn when Robert stuck his head inside. "Tom's here to take over the stock duties while we're gone. Do you want to make a final check on the pack supplies?"

"I did that last night. Everything's in order."

They ran through the usual pretrek check list until both were satisfied. Robert had built his reputation as a guide by providing superior service behind the scenes, omitting no details that could make his treks a success.

"I guess that's it," he said finally. He looked at his watch. "They should be arriving soon. Are you ready, yourself?" His brief inspection of her was just a shade critical.

Jacqui glanced down. She was wearing her customary worn jeans, a plain khaki shirt, a windbreaker that had seen better days, and scuffed boots she hadn't bothered to polish. She shrugged. "I'm not changing into anything fancier than this, if that's what you mean. They can take me as they find me."

Robert refrained from commenting on the fact that usually she didn't wear her oldest outfit on the first trek of the season. "Well, let's get the horses ready to load on the vans. I'd like to be set to go as soon as Treherne and Dantine show up."

The horses pranced a bit in the crisp morning air. "You're looking forward to this a lot more than I am," Jacqui muttered as she slid a horse blanket onto the roan gelding's back. Muscles rippled beneath the smooth hide. Her hand lingered for a moment, absorbing the latent strength and power in the animal.

Like Zane. The thought pushed its way into the forefront of her mind, together with some disturbing images: Zane riding up the hill after her... his strong hands on her arms, holding her...comforting her. His eyes, compassionate and caring... She shuddered and pushed away the images. *I've got to stop thinking about him. Last night was bad enough.*

She hadn't slept well. Until far into the small hours, she'd lain awake thinking about Zane saying the trek would be just a beginning for them. Finally she'd thrown off the covers and gone to the window, opening it wide to the night air in an attempt to cool her heated body. The shock of the bracing air through her cotton nightgown had helped; her thoughts clarified and she came to a decision. She'd simply ignore both Zane's words and the determination he'd shown. She was in charge of her life now, and it was going to stay that way. He couldn't make her do anything that she didn't want to do, so there was nothing to worry about.

Or was there? The question had echoed in her troubled dreams through the rest of the night.

Now, in the morning light, the echo had become as loud as a bull moose's cry. Nothing to worry about? If it wasn't so serious, she'd laugh and then cry at the trap she found herself in. In a few minutes, she'd be playing guide-hostess to the two men in the world she had most reason to be wary of. One man she had good reason to hate, and the other—God help her—she seemed to be obsessed by him. Why else would a part of her be crying inside at the idea of sending him away forever at the end of the week?

"Yo, Jacqui!" Robert's voice hailed her. "Here they come."

She heard the crunch of wheels on gravel as the limousine from Sun Valley Lodge pulled around the side of the cabin to the corral area. Her hand tightened on the pack strap she was adjusting. She took in a deep, slow breath. *Okay, this is it. Play it cool.*

"Are you okay, Jacqui?" Robert asked in an undertone as they moved together toward their arriving guests.

"I'm fine." She thrust her hands into the pockets of her windbreaker and came to a halt a few feet from the limousine. The air seemed thin and hard to breathe.

Zane got out of the car first. He was dressed as casually as he'd dressed the other day, only now with the addition of a quilted down vest to ward off the morning chill. He looked over at her, and she felt a tremor somewhere deep inside. For a second, she thought she saw sympathy in his expression as he waited for her glance to shift to the man now climbing out of the back seat.

Benjamin Treherne was shorter than she remembered, and much older looking. His shoulders sagged a little, like a man who was feeling a bit weary, even at seven o'clock in the morning. Only his eyes, sharply penetrating under shaggy white eyebrows, revealed the man she knew him to be—tough, ready for any battle. He came to a stop a few feet away. In a quietly neutral voice, he said, "Hello, Jacqui. I'm very glad to see you."

Everyone waited for her to reply. Out of the corner of her eye she saw that Robert looked anxious, and that Zane's gaze was practically compelling her to respond. *But I can't say "hello," "welcome," or any of those things; I can't be that much of a hypocrite!* She compromised by simply nodding in response to Benjamin's greeting. "You're here in good time," she said, her voice abrupt and a little harsh in her own ears. "We're loaded up and ready to go. Shall we get started? We have a forty-five minute drive to the trailhead."

She wheeled around and headed for the first of the two horse vans. Let Robert tell them who was riding where, she told herself, biting her lip. She'd done as much as she could. She jumped into the cab and sat with her hands clenched on the steering wheel, waiting.

It was Zane who climbed in beside her. Instantly the cab was filled with an aura of tension she could almost feel. Still without speaking, she slammed the clutch into gear and the van started off. From behind, she heard the scramble of hooves as the horses protested the sudden motion.

"Are you going to try and cut that forty-five minutes to thirty?" Zane asked dryly. "You don't have to take your temper out on the horses."

She forced her nerves to steady and flicked him a cool glance. "You can leave the driving to me. I know what I'm doing."

"I wonder. Would it have killed you to say hello to BJ, back there in the corral?"

"Don't push me, Zane. This trip isn't going to work if you do."

"It's not going to work if you can't give Benjamin the same courtesy you'd give any stranger who'd booked a trip. This is damned hard on him, you know. I told you he wasn't well."

"If he's not well, he shouldn't have come," she shot at him. She added with irony, "But of course, we both know there's nothing really wrong with his health."

"What are you talking about?"

"I saw him fishing the day before yesterday. He didn't move like a sick man, and he certainly didn't talk like one. He didn't see me, so he probably thinks I'm still fooled by your strategic play on the heart-strings."

"I only wish you were right." Zane's response was curt. "He's ill, all right, though he can still get around pretty well if he's careful. One of the valves in his heart has always been weak; lately it's begun deteriorating. It's no act, believe me."

He'd turned halfway around in his seat to speak to her. One of his arms stretched along the back of the front seat; with the other he made a gesture that started out as an appeal, but ended up as a clenched fist on his thigh.

She noted the fist and resisted the appeal. "It sounds like something you might see on the late show. I don't buy it."

"Just take a good look at him when we get started. All that's keeping him going is pills and determination."

"I can believe the determination. He's certainly persistent, even when he has to know he's wasting his time."

Silence followed her quick response. She felt a prickling sensation begin to build around her nape and knew he was staring at her. Finally he said, "I told BJ I figured you were an intelligent woman. It seems I may have to revise that opinion."

Stung, she threw him a scornful glance. "Come off it, Zane. I've agreed to do my part on this trip, and I will. It won't be any easier if we keep on taking pot-shots at each other. A trek like this requires cooperation to be successful."

"Can you promise to treat Benjamin with at least basic courtesy?"

"If you mean will I be a hypocrite, the answer is no. I'll do my best, that's all I can promise. But, dammit, give me some time—don't crowd me!''

They finished the rest of the journey to the trailhead in silence. Robert arrived only a few minutes later. Buddy jumped down from the cab; he'd been seated next to the window, with Benjamin taking the middle seat. Jacqui felt a pang; she'd completely forgotten Buddy.

While Zane went to talk to Benjamin, she waited for the dog to bound over to her. "I'm sorry, old fellow," she said, bending over him affectionately to ruffle the fur behind his ears. "I didn't mean to forget you. I'm going to need all my friends on this trip.''

Buddy frolicked around her as she went to help Robert unload the horses. He knew well enough he'd have to behave once they got on the trail. She busied herself saddling the nearest horse, the same one that Zane had ridden two days before. She was about to heave the saddle up onto its back when Zane suddenly appeared at her side.

"I'll do that," he said shortly. He grasped the saddle, his hand sliding close to hers, and she let it go as though the leather were hot metal. But she didn't move away. This close to him, she could see the slight roughness from his morning shave on the skin beneath his chin and the lines tracing outward from the narrowed corners of his eyes. His mouth—

She caught her breath sharply, then moved to the next horse. Her cheeks felt hot. *How am I going to deal with this?* she wondered. *It's almost as bad as it was six years ago. I can't let him do this to me!*

Paradoxically Jacqui's agitation over the effect Zane was having on her made it easier to handle her next encounter with Benjamin. She led a saddled mare over to him. "This is Bess," she said as she handed him the reins. "Robert picked her out for you—you told him you wanted an easy mount. If you'll climb up, I'll check the stirrup lengths for you."

As he mounted, she made herself really look at him, as Zane had suggested. *He seems fit enough for a man in his sixties,* she argued with herself. His color was good, and the slightly weary look around his eyes was probably due to the early rising hour. It was hard to reconcile her picture of him as a corporate shark, keen-eyed and devious, with the slightly rumpled, casually dressed man now smiling wryly down at her. As he waited for her to adjust a stirrup, his frank appraisal of her gave her an uncomfortably tight sensation in her chest.

"Thanks," he said as she stepped back. "I appreciate your help with the stirrups. It's been a while since I've spent much time on a horse."

"You'll do all right on Bess. She knows the trail almost as well as Robert and me."

"It's not just your help with the horse that I want to thank you for, Jacqui. It means a lot to me that you agreed to come on this trip." The quiet words were uttered unexpectedly and caught her off guard.

She searched for a reply, but could only say, "Yes, well, I'd better mount up myself."

She was riding the roan gelding that day. Her hands shook as she gathered the reins in her hands and mounted. She glanced across at Zane and saw that he was watching her closely, seeing her vulnerability...

"Let's get moving, Robert!" she cried, and dug her heels into the gelding's sides.

The morning's promise of a beautiful day was fulfilled during the first couple of hours on the trail. Spring had come early to the Sawtooths that year; there was a general greening of every bit of ground that could host grass or wildflower, and only a few snowy patches showed in the sheltered places beneath fallen logs or under the overhang of a granite ledge. The air warmed quickly, and they soon shed their jackets and vests.

Robert, now in the lead with Benjamin following, sat half turned in his saddle. He threw explanatory comments back to the others from time to time, as was his custom on a trek. Here in the territory he loved best, Robert could be almost loquacious. "You saw how the road ended back there at the trailhead, Mr. Treherne? The only way to see the interior of the Sawtooth wilderness is on foot or horseback, just like the Indians and trappers did a century and a half ago. Of course, we won't be able to get much beyond the foothills at this time of year. The snowpack hasn't melted enough yet, higher up."

"Why don't you call me Benjamin? Or BJ, like Zane does. The 'Mr.' business doesn't fit out here."

Benjamin's genial tone struck the right note with Robert. He smiled back and said, "Anything you want to know about the country around here, just ask."

"Well, now that you mention it, I would like to know where we're headed."

"See the blue smudge on that ridge in the distance? That's Pine Top Ridge. We should reach it in about two or three days, depending on how fast we travel. There's a lake tucked away up there that should be clear of ice by now. We might even find some early trout if you'd like to get in some fishing."

The men began to discuss the finer points of lake fishing. Jacqui, who'd heard it all many times before, was much more conscious of Zane, who'd slowed his horse enough so that she was forced to join him or come to a dead stop.

She braced herself, prepared for him to again raise the subject of her treatment of Benjamin. But Zane surprised her by asking instead, "Is it true they called you Sister Wolf when you were a kid?"

She blinked at the new direction his question had taken. "Yes, a few people used to call me that. How did you—"

"BJ told me." He lounged in the saddle, relaxed and in control, just as if he were riding in an easy chair. "I can see how the name would fit. I doubt many people would ever have called you a tame creature, even when you were a child."

It was easier to resist the attraction she felt toward him by thrusting him away. "Then you'd be smart to tread carefully with me, Zane. Wolves are wary beasts. They've had some bad experiences with men who hunt them down."

"Are they as wary with their own kind? Wolves do find each other and mate, don't they, Sister Wolf?"

She gave him a haughty stare and, not deigning to answer, started to push the gelding ahead. "No, wait," he said, stopping her. "I'm sorry—that was more provocative than I meant it to be."

She eyed him warily. "I think you say pretty much what you intend to say."

"What I should have said was that I find the subject of wolves interesting. You studied them, didn't you?"

His candid expression was disarming. Deliberately so, she suspected. She responded anyway. "Yes, along with other species of wildlife."

"I knew you were in Canada this past winter, on a field trip. Did you see any wolves there?"

"Not as many as I'd like to have seen." She wondered how he'd known about the trip. Years ago it had been his apparently genuine interest in her studies that had thawed her resistance to him as Benjamin's emissary. In her pleasure at having such an exciting man take an interest in her, she'd been able to forget that he was only asking for the sake of the reports he was supposed to make. Later she'd believed he really was interested because of her. Now it seemed he'd been keeping track of her still. Curious, she asked, "How did you know about my trip to Canada?"

"I spoke with one of your professors a few days ago, when I was trying to locate you. He also mentioned you were returning home early."

Her eyes narrowed. "You must have been persuasive—the faculty aren't usually so forthcoming to a casual inquiry."

"Ah, but my inquiry wasn't casual." She saw the glint in his eye and guessed that an overworked professor at a busy university would be easy prey for a man like Zane.

They came to a rougher portion of the trail, and for a few minutes there was no opportunity to talk. But as soon as the path cleared again, he dropped back and said, "Tell me more about the trip to Canada. Were there many students involved?"

In spite of her determination to keep up her guard against him, he somehow got around her with questions that put her on her mettle; he had a quick intel-

ligence and seemed genuinely interested in what she
had to tell him. Caught up in her own love for com-
municating wildlife lore, she gradually relaxed.

When a chittering, scrambling sound came from
overhead, they both looked up. A pair of squirrels,
intent on a quarrel over a pine nut, almost fell off their
perch on a tree branch. When they became aware of
the riders just below them, their dismay was comical.
Pine nut forgotten, they raced up the tree trunk and
out of sight.

Jacqui burst out laughing, and heard Zane's deeper
chuckle blend in. Eyes sparkling, she glanced at him,
ready to make a comment. Instead she drew in a sharp
breath and her smile disappeared. His gray eyes
seemed to smolder as he looked at her; his gaze was
fixed on her mouth. Somehow his horse had moved
closer, so close that he would only have to lean over a
little bit to... Her heart leaped into her throat, and she
blurted, "We'd better catch up with the others—
there's a view up ahead that Robert always likes to
show off."

It was a good five minutes before her insides calmed
down again. The spectacular view kept them lingering for a good half hour while the horses rested. The
stop was only one of many along the way that morning. Their midday picnic lunch lasted nearly two
hours. It was the slowest pace they'd ever kept during
the summers she'd worked with Robert.

Benjamin seemed to be enjoying himself very much.
After lunch, while they lazed beneath a shady tree, he
kept asking for more of Robert's anecdotes about his
experiences as a wilderness guide. His interest and
questions seemed inexhaustible. Jacqui frowned,
guessing that he probably approached a corporate

takeover with the same thoroughness. Apparently he couldn't turn that part of himself off, even here. Finally Robert responded to one query by saying, "It's too bad you can't ask Jacqui's grandfather about tracking animals in the woods. He was a real expert."

"I already know about Jim Littlewolf's expertise." Surprised by Benjamin's statement, Jacqui looked up. She watched him pull a pipe out of his pocket, then after contemplating the empty bowl regretfully, content himself with smoothing the well-worn finish with his thumb. "Jim took me on a trip down the Salmon River once, along that stretch you call the River of No Return. It was one of the most beautiful and scary experiences in my life."

Curiosity made Jacqui break the silence she'd mostly maintained toward Benjamin. "I thought you only came here because of your mine. I didn't realize you and Gramps spent that much time together."

Benjamin gave her one of his keen-eyed looks, then smiled. "He looked me up soon after I first arrived. He didn't like the idea of the mines opening up again in this part of Idaho; he was sure we'd wreck the environment." Benjamin turned to Zane and explained, "I learned later that he used to lobby any politicians who came through these parts on hunting or fishing trips; he supported the idea of putting all the land into the National Park system. I always suspected it was due to Jim as much as anyone that Congress finally passed the Act that established the Sawtooths as a protected wilderness area."

Jacqui listened in some confusion as he went on talking to the others about Jim Littlewolf's exploits both as a woodsman and a wily diplomat. If she didn't know better, she might have thought Benjamin understood how his revelation had shaken her, and that he wanted to give her time to recover.

How many other things don't I know about Benjamin Treherne and his dealings with my family? she wondered. Her grandfather, like her mother, had usually avoided talking about anything having to do with Benjamin and his mine, and of the circumstances of her father's death. It was almost as though they'd had a tacit agreement to protect her. Sensing their reluctance, she'd never pressed them. But their silence hadn't helped her.

Now she sighed, feeling the futility of thinking about the past. Her glance fell on Buddy, who was lolling on a grassy space in the sun with his tongue hanging out, panting. He was looking up, his eyes fixed almost adoringly on Zane, who had launched into a humorous account of his own first trip on white water rapids. The dog followed Zane's gestures as though fascinated.

You too, Buddy? she thought. She felt a pang from Buddy's apparent desertion, even though she suspected that the dog's switch of interest had more to do with the fact that his former owner, a Canadian trapper, had had a voice similar to Zane's—deep and confident. Though not quite as rich, perhaps, or as magnetic...

She saw where her thoughts were leading her and pulled herself back just in time. She scrambled to her feet and broke into the conversation. "Shouldn't we get going, Robert? We have a few miles to go before we reach our camping spot for tonight."

Robert surprised her by saying, "We're in no real rush, Jacqui. Why don't we call it a day and set up camp right here?" To Zane and Benjamin, he said,

"There's a small lake about a hundred yards off the trail. The water supply will come in handy tonight and in the morning. We can loaf around, have an early supper and watch the sunset."

About to object that there was another two hour's daylight for riding, and just as good a water supply at the other camp, Jacqui refrained when she saw the relieved expression on Benjamin's face. She'd seen he was tired, of course—that was usual with most people on the first day of the week-long trek. But now she saw that his color wasn't as good as it had been earlier. And he looked more than just tired; he look exhausted.

Zane stood and stretched, then said, "Sounds like a good idea to me. Where shall we set up our tents?"

"I'll start unloading the packhorses," Jacqui said. Her forehead creased in a slight frown as she walked to the clearing where they'd left the horses to graze.

At various times during the day, she'd observed Benjamin when he wasn't aware she was watching him. Apart from making a joke or two about the effects of riding on a man of sedentary habits, he'd made no real complaint. Yet it was clear that roughing it wasn't his customary way of life. And maybe there was some truth to what Zane had said about his health. *He's doing all this just for the chance to see me—and on my own terms, too. Why? Why does it matter so much to him?*

They set up the tents in a protected spot not far from an old fire ring, a circle of fire-blackened rocks in a flat area of hard-packed dirt. "Ordinarily we wouldn't build a fire," Robert explained as he carried over an armful of broken chunks of wood. "We pack in a camp stove and fuel. But I found a deadfall over by that crag; it needs clearing out anyway, so I thought we might as well have a real fire tonight.''

They worked at a leisurely pace. Benjamin ambled around the camp, helping a little here and there. He didn't go out of his way to avoid speaking to her, but he didn't make any demands on her, either. He seemed willing to let her adjust to the situation at her own pace. Her inner confusion increased; he just wasn't behaving at all in the way she'd expected him to.

After sharing in the light snack, which was all anyone wanted for supper, Benjamin retired early to his tent, making a joke about his stiff muscles, but promising to be up bright and early the next morning. Robert went off to check on the horses. Zane and Jacqui were left alone together in the afterglow of sunset.

Jacqui sat on the ground near the small camp fire with her legs drawn up in front of her, looking into the flames. She could practically feel Zane's gaze resting on her. If she turned her head to look at him, she knew she'd see in his eyes a disturbing reminder of all the things she was trying so hard to ignore.

She clasped her arms around her knees and fought to keep from turning her head. *Ignoring him doesn't work,* she thought. *Somehow I'm going to have to come to terms with the way he can affect me so easily. If only he wouldn't keep looking at me the way he does!*

Zane quietly got up and put another piece of wood on the fire. He saw the quick tensing of Jacqui's body as he briefly came closer to her. He hesitated, then settled back into his former position.

It bothers her when I get close, he thought, his gaze resting on her again. She wasn't wearing her hair in a braid today; she'd tied it back in a loose knot at her nape. Several strands had broken free to curl forward over her cheek. Her head was tilted forward as she watched the fire; he could see the vulnerable curve of her neck.

"When I saw you in Ketchum the other day," he said, breaking the silence to help control the urge he felt to touch her, "your hair was wrapped around your head like a crown. It turned gold when the sun touched it, but now it looks as dark as those shadows down by the lake."

She looked up slowly, almost unwillingly. He saw the pale light from the sky reflected in her eyes, turning the green of her irises a shade bluer. The triangular shape of her face, together with the unusual shape of her eyes, gave her the look of some wild, rare creature as she stared back at him. Beside her the fire crackled, then popped; the pungent smell of melting pine pitch rose to blend with the other scents of evening.

"Don't, Zane," she said, her voice low and a little unsteady. "Don't look at me that way."

"I like to look at you."

She made a restless movement, a protesting gesture with her hand. Unable to resist the pull he felt toward her, he reached out and caught on his finger some of the hair that curled beside her ear. A shiver rippled over her, so slight as to be almost invisible. But his own body, tuned to awareness, tightened in response. He went on, deliberately wooing her with words. "Your eyes are like no eyes I've ever seen. In this light, and in this place, they make me think of one of your wild creatures. So wary, and so beautiful."

Her eyes closed briefly, and he saw a swallowing movement in her throat. "Very pretty words, Zane. I know what I look and smell like after a hard day in the saddle. If you're looking for a wildlife comparison, I think 'badger' would be about right."

He felt a quick spurt of amusement at her attempt to turn aside his compliment. "No, not a badger. You smell like the sun, like saddle leather and pine trees. I never knew before now how erotic those scents could be."

She looked back at him, and he saw in her eyes that she was as acutely aware of him as he was of her. It was only the sounds Robert made, returning through the trees, that stopped him from taking her in his arms then and there to try to erase the doubts he saw mixed in with her awareness.

"Jacqui, I think we should—"

Before he could go on, she jumped to her feet and grabbed a leather bucket from the supplies stacked nearby. She called out, "We'll need more water in the morning, Rob. I'll get some now before it gets dark." When Zane started to rise, she said hastily, "No, don't get up. I don't need any help."

Zane got up, anyway, and stood with his legs braced, watching her vanish down the path to the lake. Robert came up to the fire ring and dumped his arm load of wood on the ground. After another moment, the younger man cleared his throat and said, "Jacqui's had a tough day."

"Yes." Zane's gaze was still fixed on the path to the lake.

"It isn't easy for her, what with the way she feels about her uncle and all." Robert's expression was troubled when Zane finally glanced over at him. "She doesn't need any more complications."

Zane's eyes narrowed, and for a moment he debated whether to answer the unspoken message in Robert's remark. Finally he said tersely, "I'm going to take a stroll down to the lake. You can come with me if you feel you need to."

Robert hesitated, then shook his head. "No, I don't think so. But I'll be here when you get back."

Zane nodded without speaking, then he turned and strode down the path toward the lake.

Chapter Five

When Jacqui reached the edge of the lake, she set the bucket down unfilled. It had only been an excuse to get away. She drew in a breath of the pine-scented air and tried to absorb the serenity around her.

The sun had disappeared behind the hills, leaving an ultramarine sky and water darkening to cobalt blue. Shadows gathered beneath the trees that bordered the lake. The lake was small, perhaps sixty yards across at this point. A giant fir tree had fallen partway down from a low bluff and lay like a jackstraw suspended over the still water. Attracted by its air of grand isolation, she walked about ten feet out on the trunk and sat down, letting her legs dangle over the water.

When Zane arrived, his step on the end of the log was light, almost soundless. She looked at him and he paused, as though silently waiting to see if she'd send him away. She didn't, and he said quietly, "Better get a grip on something. I'm coming out."

Jacqui curled her hand around the broken stub of a branch for support as the fallen tree dipped a little under Zane's weight. Her gaze stayed on him as he moved toward her, balancing on the rough bark with the surefootedness of a cat. She felt a sense of inevitability in his coming; had she known he would when she'd hurried away from their too-intense exchange by the fire?

"You could have put us both in the water, coming out here," she remarked. "Are you thinking you might like to take an ice-water bath?"

He adjusted his position to face her. "Not tonight, thank you. What are you doing sitting here by yourself?"

"Enjoying the evening show from my box seat. If you'll be very still, you can see some of the main actors. Look over there on the far side, just below that red pine."

He was silent for a moment, then she saw him nod when he sighted the arrowlike disturbance in the mirror stillness of the water's surface. A small head protruded from the water just at the point of the moving arrow. Two smaller arrows followed. In a low tone he asked, "What are they?"

"A family of beavers. See? There they go, up the bank. The wind direction is toward us—they don't know we're here. And I saw a pair of deer just a few moments ago. We may see them again. I'm sure they're still around."

The moments slipped by as they watched and listened to the comings and goings of the evening population of the lake. It was a busy world, especially during the changing hour of twilight when day creatures made room for night creatures. Jacqui glanced frequently at the man sitting beside her. He was totally absorbed in the show and quick to pick up on the silent signals she gave him from time to time. He was first to spot the peregrine falcon that circled briefly over the lake before vanishing into the sky again. When the pair of deer returned like shadows to sip daintily from the lake, he looked at Jacqui and smiled. His smile slipped through her guard as easily as the falcon had slipped through the air. In spite of herself, she felt a kinship of spirit with Zane that she'd never known with anyone else. At that moment, she knew she'd remember this brief half hour of shared harmony for the rest of her life.

Her hand tightened on the branch stub, and she welcomed the rough sensation of the bark pressing into her palm. Something inside her protested, *How can I keep up my guard against him when it feels so right, being here with him like this?* She shifted on her perch, seeking a comfort that wasn't available. The log swayed gently.

"Easy does it," he said, breaking the silence at last. "Or it'll be you who puts us in the water."

"You're very good at being quiet." Her voice sounded husky in her own ears. "That's a quality many people don't have—they're uncomfortable with silence."

"You and I haven't had many opportunities to be quiet together."

"No." She looked away, remembering too well the clashes that had made some of their former meetings anything but peaceful. Nor was the moment peaceful now. She felt charged with emotion, volatile. She sensed that Zane, too, was less casual than he appeared—for all his relaxed manner as he balanced on the log, one foot nearly trailing in the water.

"We should go back," she said, and heard the lack of conviction behind the words.

"Not yet. A few minutes more."

It was the knowledge that he, too, was feeling something of what she was feeling that kept her still. But she knew it was a risk, staying here alone with him. *I was right,* she thought. *It's Zane who's the danger to me on this trip, not Benjamin.*

"Jacqui, I want to thank you."

She looked at him, startled. "Why?"

"For how you handled yourself today with BJ."

"I didn't do anything special."

"It was hard on you. I could see it in your face. Before, I just thought you were being stubborn."

A piece of bark came off in her hand. She looked at it without really seeing it, then tossed it into the water. "It wasn't as bad as I expected."

"Are you still angry with me for pressuring you into coming?"

There was a note in his voice that let her know her answer was important to him. Slowly she shook her head. "Perhaps I should be, but no, I'm not angry now. Robert said I'd made a bogeyman out of Benjamin, and maybe I had. I want to put the past behind me, and this trek may be the best way to accomplish that."

"And after that? What do you want to make of your life, Jacqui?"

Surprised, she looked at him. "To make it count for something, I suppose. Maybe to feel like something I've done has made life a little better for someone besides myself. A little happiness, contentment." She paused, and her mouth twisted wryly. "That sounds like I'm asking a lot, doesn't it?"

"Sounds like a pretty good blueprint to me."

The quiet tones of his voice set up a yearning inside her that she could no longer resist. Impulsively she asked, "Zane, haven't you ever wondered what it would be like to go off on your own—to give up working for Benjamin?"

"I can't say that I have. Why do you ask?"

"You're an intelligent man, and from what I've picked up here and there, highly skilled at what you do. You could work anywhere, for anyone. Maybe even have your own business. Why don't you?"

"TMC is one of the top corporations in the world. My work is interesting, often challenging. Why should I go elsewhere?"

"Because you can never be your own man, working for Benjamin." In her eagerness to convince, she leaned toward him. "You're a man who should be giving orders, not taking them."

He glanced down at her hand, resting on the rough bark inches away from his thigh. "I'm gratified that you have such a high opinion of me."

She bit her lip, regretting the impulse that had made her speak. "It was just a thought."

"I think it was more than that." He reached for her hand, taking it into his before she could withdraw it. A shiver of awareness streaked up her arm and through her body. With his gaze intent on her face, he said, "Tell me, Jacqui, have you thought about what I said to you the other night when you came to my room?"

"If you're referring to our having some kind of relationship after the trek, of course I've thought about it." She had to stop and draw breath. His thumb stroked the back of her hand in circular movements, distracting her. "But I still feel the same way. It's a mistake to think there can ever be anything between us."

"Especially as long as I go on working for TMC, isn't that what you really mean?"

"That isn't it, at least not entirely. We don't have anything in common—our lives and goals are too different."

"I don't agree. I think we both recognized six years ago that we have a great deal in common. I haven't been able to forget you in all that time, and I don't think you've forgotten, either."

She drew her hand from his light hold and with an effort said, "This conversation isn't going anywhere, Zane."

"Only because you don't want it to—not yet, anyway." His voice seemed deeper, richer. "But I'm a patient man, Jacqui. I can wait."

Though the light was now fading fast, she could see the glittering expression of promise in his eyes. Her heartbeat quickened. "Don't waste your time, Zane. Or mine. I meant what I said. I'm not looking for an involvement."

His smile quirked the corner of his mouth. "Neither of us may have been looking, Jacqui. But I think the involvement has found us anyway. And if you deny that you're not feeling something for me right now, I'll know you're lying."

"That's only physical chemistry," she retorted. Appalled that he could see through her defenses so easily, her inward agitation increased. "It means nothing in the long run."

"It means a hell of a lot, but that's not all we've got going for us—or what we could have, if we gave it a chance."

"Name one thing we have in common," she challenged him.

"Strength. We both have it. You don't like being thwarted in what you want any more than I do. And you usually get your way, don't you?"

"That's hardly enough to base a relationship on!"

"In many ways, we're both loners. You've walked alone a good deal of your life, haven't you? I saw it in your eyes the first time I met you, when you were only sixteen."

"You'll have to work hard to make me believe you've been lonely, Zane. In all your travels, I'm sure there've been plenty of women eager to keep you company."

No sooner had the words slipped from her, than she wished she could call them back. *I don't like thinking of him with other women,* she realized as shock spread through her. Aloud, she hastily amended her words, "Not that your love life is any of my business, of course. What I mean to say—"

He interrupted her before she could get into a worse tangle. "What you mean to say is that you're still determined to deny what's between you and me, right now."

She grabbed hold of the stub and got to her feet, swaying a little to catch her balance. "That's it exactly. Right now, I'm more concerned with what's between us and dry land—it's almost dark, in case you haven't noticed."

In one smooth movement, he rose to his feet also. "Oh, I've noticed. I thought you hadn't."

Chagrined, she shot him a glance and exclaimed, "Let's go, then."

They'd just reached the end of the tree where it slanted across the water's edge when Buddy came bounding out of the shadows. With a deep "Woof!" he jumped on the tree trunk and tried to thrust past Zane to reach Jacqui.

"Watch it!" Zane exclaimed. Jacqui grabbed at him to keep her balance. They both slipped and a second later Jacqui was sitting waist deep in shallow water, pushing at Buddy, trying to keep him from submerging her completely as he bounced around excitedly.

"Buddy, get back!" she exclaimed, gasping from the shock of the icy water. "I'm not drowning, but I will be if you don't stop jumping on me! Go on back to camp!" Her shove and sharp tone sent him on his way, chastened.

"Oh, Lord," she muttered, and wiped the water out of her eyes. "Zane? Where are you?"

"Right behind you."

She twisted around. Zane was standing knee-deep in the water, grinning at her. He'd fared better than she had; he hadn't fallen in completely. He said, "I hope the beavers appreciate our contribution to the show tonight."

Zane reached for her hand to pull her up, and they waded ashore. A stone turned under Jacqui's foot; she stumbled and fell against him. He caught her close—so close she could hear the sound of his uneven breathing. Her throat went dry, and she stared at him wordlessly. Her heart pounded, not from the shock of their fall into the icy water, but from the gathering of her feelings into one great tumultuous mass inside her—feelings that had been building in her all day. She

gave a smothered exclamation and didn't resist when
he wrapped his arms around her even more tightly.

"You're soaking wet. We should go up by the
fire…get warm." Zane's voice sounded a little slurred.

"Yes…" Her breath came faster; adrenaline turned
into liquid fire that built inside her and ran through
her veins. It seemed so natural to raise her hands and
place them on his chest, then to slide them upward
around his neck. "This is crazy," she protested, more
to herself than to him. "It doesn't mean anything—it's
only chemistry."

"You may be right." His eyes were very bright, even
in the gathering darkness. "But you have to agree it's
one hell of a way to get warm…"

And then his lips found hers, and the faint light of
the stars appearing in the heavens and reflected in the
waters around them seemed to whirl into a kaleido-
scope of flickering bits of light. She held on tight and
closed her eyes, but the lights still seemed to whirl inside her, dazzling her.

And then something deep inside her struggled hard
to break free…to take control. It was like that first
time six years before, only more powerful. *It feels so
right to be in Zane's arms,* she thought, dazed. And
then she stopped thinking and gave herself up to the
sensations that were bombarding her on all fronts. He
tasted of citronella and lake water dampness and his
own elusive taste; his lips and tongue moving on her
lips caused them to open hungrily for him. She pressed
against him, a small moan of frustration escaping her
because their soaked clothes hampered her; her hands
on his shoulders could get no purchase on the wet ny-
lon of his down vest.

He groaned, too, then released her long enough to cup her face in his hands. "Jacqui...you're right, this is crazy, here, like this—"

Caught in an upwelling of passion greater than any she'd ever felt before, Jacqui put both hands behind his neck and pulled his head down to her again. "I know, but don't say it! Not now. Just kiss me again—"

They swayed together, and for a little while longer it was possible not to feel the rising breeze that cut through the air and their wet clothes with knifelike sharpness. The lonely hoot of an owl somewhere in the distance threaded its lost sound through the air around them. But Jacqui was far more conscious of the slightly rough texture of Zane's jaw where it touched hers, of the thick coarse feel of his hair curling around her fingers and of the intimacy of their bodies pressing together so urgently. Most of all, she was intoxicated by the fusing of their mouths and tongues in a kiss that seemed to go on forever.

Then finally, it was too much. Her heightened senses overloaded, and she began to shiver convulsively. When he realized her shaking wasn't due to passion, Zane broke the kiss.

"Jacqui—you're freezing." He wrapped his arms around her more tightly, only this time for protection.

"Of c-course I'm freezing. I'm also very em— em—"

"Very what?"

"Embarrassed. After all I said—Zane, I didn't mean for that to happen." Guilt from her betraying emotions made her shake all the harder.

"There's nothing to be embarrassed about. It happened to both of us. Come on, let's get back to camp."

They hurried up the path. Zane held on to her, keeping her tucked in what shelter he could give her with his body. When they came out of the dark into the circle of light around the fire, Robert looked up, then started to his feet.

"Good Lord, what happened?"

"B-buddy came along and jumped us just as we were coming off a log on the l-lake," she chattered.

"Well, you'd both better change into dry clothes while I build up the fire."

Grateful that Robert didn't mention that Buddy had returned to camp a good ten minutes before and was now curled up near the fire, Jacqui hurried to her tent to recover.

What happened to me? she marveled as she stripped off her wet jeans and tossed them in a heap beside her sleeping bag. *One minute I was standing there in the water and the next I was holding on to him like he was the last man on earth.* Chemistry wasn't enough to explain it. She'd been driven by a surge of need so strong, that even now she couldn't analyze it. It hadn't mattered that the arguments she'd given him only moments before had vanished from her thoughts like smoke in a strong breeze. Breeze? No; it had been a storm, a storm she hadn't been able to control.

She dragged a sweater over her head, then reached for a thick cardigan. *Now calm down,* she ordered herself as she buttoned the cardigan with shaking fingers. *It wasn't that bad. You're not out of control— you were just upset. It was harder on you today than you thought, dealing with Benjamin and the whole situation. You're off balance; Zane's stirred you up a lot these past few days. It will pass.*

Finally fortified by her own arguments and well bundled up in dry jeans, two sweaters and her spare windbreaker, she forced herself to lift the tent flap and go outside again.

"Here—see if this will warm you up." Robert handed her a large mug filled with steaming hot tea. "I put a little something extra in it. You don't want to come down with a chill or worse."

After one quick glance, she avoided looking directly at Zane. That one glance had shown her that he wasn't going to let her forget what had happened down by the lake. The muscles in her legs tensed for flight, but she resisted the feeling. She'd allowed her instincts to betray her too much already tonight. Taking a deep breath, she cupped her hands around the tea and moved to stand with apparent casual ease beside the crackling fire.

She almost dropped her cup when Robert asked, "Where's the water bucket, Jacqui? I don't see it anywhere."

"Uh—I dropped it down by the lake. I'll get it in the morning."

Before Robert could say anything more, Zane broke in with a question about the route for the following day, distracting him. But she could see Robert's curiosity hadn't been satisfied. While Zane kept up a conversation with him, she was conscious of Robert's glances frequently returning to her face. She drank the rest of her tea in as short a time as possible, then declared her intention of retiring for the night. "It must be the 'something extra' you put in the tea, Rob, but I'm sleepy as an owl at noontime."

Turning away, her glance was caught by Zane's. He smiled, and she knew he was remembering, as she was, the owl that had hooted during the kiss down by the lake.

"Good night," she said hastily, and disappeared into her tent.

The next morning, Jacqui awoke later than the others. Bundled in her sleeping bag, she lay for a few moments, blinking while she reoriented herself. A burst of laughter from outside brought her fully awake. She was on the trek...Robert and Zane and Benjamin were outside...and last night she'd had trouble falling asleep because...

She groaned and ducked her head back inside the sleeping bag. Last night she'd made a major tactical error. She'd given in to the feelings Zane had stirred up in her; she'd let him see how much he affected her.

What would he do about the advantage she'd handed him? He'd made it plain enough that he anticipated having a relationship with her at the end of the trip. Now, by behaving so foolishly, she'd just made everything ten times more difficult for herself. How on earth could she regain the ground she'd lost?

The smell of frying bacon reached her nostrils. Reluctantly she dressed and went outside. Robert was busy over the camp stove.

"Hi," he said. "Help yourself to coffee. The rest will be ready in a minute."

"It smells good," she said, even though at the moment she had no appetite for the skillet full of crispy fried potatoes and scrambled eggs standing on one side of the stove. She was about to ask the whereabouts of their guests when she saw Benjamin coming up from

the lake with Buddy at his side. And Zane was—
    "Good morning."

The voice came from her right. She whirled around
and saw Zane standing beside a pine tree about six
yards away. A mirror was perched in the joint of a
convenient branch; his face was lathered on one side,
and he had a razor in his hand.

I have to tell him now, she told herself. *There might
not be a better chance all day.* Coffee cup in hand, she
walked over to him.

"How are you?" he asked. "Any ill effects from
our impromptu dunking last night?"

From the myriad of possible answers to that question, she picked the only safe reply. "I'm fine. I never
catch colds."

"That's good." He smiled at her. The expression in
his eyes was warm; he seemed to be relaxed and in very
good humor as he lifted the razor again.

As she searched for words to tell him of her feelings, she was distracted, watching him shave. She'd
seen Robert shaving, and her dad a long time ago. But
she'd never thought the masculine ritual was anything special. Now it fascinated her to watch Zane as
he tilted his jaw just so for a stroke up the vulnerable
area beneath his chin; how he narrowed his eyes and
stretched his upper lip to shave the short space beneath his nose. He skipped a dot of white shaving
cream beneath his ear, and she had to restrain herself
from pointing it out to him.

His eyes caught hers in the mirror's reflection, and
he smiled again. "I could let my beard grow this week,
but shaving's too much of a habit with me."

She nodded, unable to speak. In their little pocket
of intimacy, watching him shave, she saw in the shared

homey act the very essence of all the love and caring that was possible between a man and a woman. *Love isn't just chemistry,* she thought with sudden clarity. *It's all the small things, the daily things, shared by two people making a life together. Like this moment right now with Zane.*

The hand holding her coffee cup was clenched so tight it hurt. *I can't be in love with Zane,* she argued with herself. Just days ago she'd only thought of him with bitterness and anger, if she thought of him at all. How could her feelings change so suddenly, reverse so completely?

They can't, she told herself with painful force. *This is all just a mirage... an illusion.*

She must have closed her eyes, because she opened them to find his gaze in the mirror fixed on her. He wiped his face with his towel and turned to face her. Quietly he asked again, "Are you all right?"

For a moment, she couldn't reply. She swallowed to ease her dry throat, then said, "Listen, Zane, about last night... what happened between us was a mistake." She saw his frown appear and went on, her words tumbling out. "I have my life all planned. There's no room in it for... for diversions."

The murmur of voices came to her from behind, and conscious they could be interrupted at any moment, she said, "I admit I had a crush on you years ago, Zane. Those feelings... I suppose they had to come out, just once. But that's all it was. You can see that, can't you?"

"And what about my feelings? What explanation do you have for those?"

She looked at him helplessly. "It isn't real for you, either. You were curious, perhaps, or maybe a little challenged by the way I've treated you. But you don't really want an involvement with me any more than I do with you. It's simply impossible!''

As their eyes locked, turmoil in her expression, stubborn resistance in his, they were interrupted. Benjamin called over, ''Hey, you two—breakfast's ready. Are you coming?''

''In a minute.'' Zane called back. His gaze didn't waver from Jacqui's.

''I mean it, Zane,'' she said hurriedly. ''Please don't try to pick up from where we left off last night. I have all I can handle dealing with Benjamin. I can't handle an emotional tangle with you, too!''

He lifted the towel in his hand and wiped away the last of the shaving cream from his face. ''Okay, Jacqui. You've made your point. Now why don't we leave it at that and have breakfast?''

She bit her lip in frustration, watching him walk away. Did he mean he agreed with her, or what? Her glance shifted, then fell on Benjamin who was standing next to the camp stove with his filled plate in his hands. Her uncle had a thoughtful expression on his face as Zane passed him with only a brief greeting, took a plate, then went to sit by himself beneath a tree. Benjamin's gaze traveled from Zane back to Jacqui.

''Good morning,'' was all he said. And then he smiled.

Chapter Six

After breakfast, while Zane was helping Benjamin dismantle his tent, Robert found a moment to speak with Jacqui privately.

"Jacqui, about last night..."

"Yes, Rob?" Warily she looked up from her task of repacking the kitchen equipment.

He looked a trifle embarrassed, but also determined. "I'm not sure what happened between you and Zane down there by the lake, and I'm not asking. But I'm here if you need me."

Her smile at him was a little crooked. "You think I might be getting in over my head? You don't have to worry about me, Rob. But I appreciate the fact that you care."

"It's my fault you got involved in this trek. Sometimes I think it was the right thing to do, then other times I'm not so sure I shouldn't have let well enough alone."

Her hands hesitated on the packing strap. For a moment she did wonder if it would have been better never to have realized how much power Zane had to affect her. "No, it's okay," she said, and firmly buckled the strap. "I talked to Zane. I've got things under control now."

She saw the dubious expression that came over Robert's face and knew he, like herself, was thinking that Zane wasn't a man to submit easily to anyone's control but his own. *And Benjamin's,* she added silently. What hold could her uncle have on a man like Zane that he could command so much loyalty from him?

"Here—this pack is ready," she said. "Give me a hand lifting it on the horse, okay?"

"Treherne is turning out to have a lot of staying power, isn't he?" Robert commented as he helped her. "And he's not a complainer, either, like some of the clients we get."

"Yes, I've noticed. I've also noticed you get along with him pretty well."

"He sure knows his stuff when it comes to business. He gave me a suggestion for calculating my profit and loss flow that should improve my credit rating at the bank. I'm going to try it when we get back."

Robert went off to take care of another task, and Jacqui was left to frown over the bit of news Robert had so innocently dropped. So Benjamin was still taking an interest in the Janek family's financial affairs, was he? Why? Was it just that he couldn't resist talking business no matter where he was, or did he have some other motive?

It could be that he was just a man who couldn't rest unless he were controlling the lives of everyone around him. He'd done it with her parents...with her through the trust fund...and now in the interest he was taking in Robert's guide service. *I may be getting paranoid over him,* she thought, *but it's just as well to remember that if I get involved with Zane, it'll mean being involved with Benjamin, too.*

When Robert called out for them to mount up, she had to resist the impulse to simply climb on the roan gelding and take off into the woods, to get away from the complex problems she felt building up around her.

Soon after they started off, Benjamin reined his horse to one side of the trail and waited for Jacqui to come up alongside. With a genial smile he said, "Do you mind if I ride along with you for a while?"

She discovered she'd been half expecting the overture. Resigned, she said, "No, I don't mind."

During the next ten minutes or so, he plied her with questions regarding the trail and the countryside. Without letting down her guard completely, she did relax somewhat. In response to one of his questions, she responded, "Yes, the name Idaho is an Indian term. It's actually 'Ed-da-how,' and it means 'light on the mountain.' You can see why, can't you?"

She pointed ahead of them; in the distance they could see soaring peaks, brilliantly lit by sunlight on white snow. Benjamin nodded. "This is beautiful country—very much the way I remember it. I'm glad I got to see it again."

Zane was riding with Robert several yards down the trail. Robert must have told him something funny just then, because he tipped his head back and his deep laugh came clearly to them. Caught by the sound,

Jacqui allowed her gaze to rest on him. Broad shouldered, lean in waist and hips, he sat on his horse with casual grace, and she wondered yet again...

"Benjamin, where did Zane learn to ride so well? He's never said, but what little accent he has sounds like he comes from the city, not the country."

"He does come from the city. As far as I know, he never saw a horse before he reached his early twenties."

She glanced over at Benjamin and saw an expression of pleased surprise in his eyes. She realized that her comment was the first completely spontaneous remark she'd made to him.

He went on, "Zane spent a year in Argentina managing a mining venture that eventually played out. While he was there, he learned just about everything there was to learn from the friends he made among the gauchos. They're—"

"Yes, I know what gauchos are," she interrupted, almost absently. Her gaze had returned to Zane and lingered. "The best riders in the world, some people say. Though I bet some of our Idaho rodeo riders could challenge that claim."

"Zane's done some rodeo riding, too. We had a few problems with a silver mine in Colorado, and—"

"Good Lord, Benjamin, is there any place you don't have a mining interest?" She reined in her horse to one side to avoid some prickly underbrush growing out into the trail.

He chuckled as he met her look of incredulity. She heard satisfaction in his voice as he said, "Well, I don't like to brag, but TMC does pretty well. It keeps both Zane and me hopping most of the time."

A frown creased her forehead. "Benjamin, I'd like to ask you something."

"Ask anything you like."

"What exactly is it that you want from me? Like you said, you're a busy man. And for all that Zane apparently likes riding for recreation, I don't think it's really your style. You wanted to see me bad enough to spend a week in the wilderness, even though you're not exactly in the best of health. So I have to ask, why?"

He paused long enough to set off prickles of uneasiness in her stomach. But when he did reply, he only said, "The main reason was that I wanted the chance to get to know you better, Jacqui." He gave her a smile that on him seemed oddly wistful. "I knew you for such a short time when you were a child. I always thought you were a special little girl, and I wanted to see for myself how you've turned out as a woman."

"Zane kept you pretty well informed about me, as I remember."

"Yes. I was very proud of you. You did so well in your studies. And I came to see you ride that year you were in the Grand National equitation finals in San Francisco. I remember how confident and poised you were, even in front of thousands of people."

"You were there?" Her surprise showed on her face. She'd been seventeen the year she'd ridden Anton's best purebred in one of the horse world's major show events. It had been a very important occasion for her. Zane had come to cheer her on, though he hadn't been able to stay afterward. Now she knew he'd probably had to leave early with Benjamin.

She was still digesting this bit of information when he said, "I was very sorry when you and I stopped being friends, Jacqui. We were good friends when you were quite small. But you probably don't remember that.''

"No, I don't." Her gaze rested on him with a troubled frown. Every memory she'd had of Benjamin from before the day of the quarrel with her father seemed to have faded completely.

It was even difficult to call up his image of eighteen years ago. She could only remember a dim confusion of loud voices and angry frowns and gestures. Somehow that scene seemed to have very little to do with the man riding beside her now. She studied him, seeing a man whose lined face showed, like scars, the effects of a lifetime's battles and disappointments.

He returned her scrutiny with a keen glance of his own, then said, "You still remember the quarrel your father and I had the day before he died, don't you?"

"Yes, I do." Her stomach tightened.

"I was always sorry you were there that day. You were too young to understand."

She pulled back on her reins, and her horse obediently came to a stop. Benjamin halted also, the leather of his saddle creaking as he shifted to keep his eyes on her while his horse backed up. Before he could speak again, she said, "I understood enough, Benjamin. Believe me, it's better if we don't bring it up now. I've managed to put the past behind me. If you stir it up, and insist on talking about what can't be changed, there can only be trouble between us."

"I'm not trying to change the past, Jacqui. I'm just trying to set it straight. And maybe make up for some of the unhappiness you've known. Won't you let me do that for you?"

She heard what sounded like genuine concern in his voice, and perhaps the echo of an old remorse, but she was determined to keep him at arm's length. She shook her head and said, "I'm doing very well now, and I've made my plans for the future. You needn't be concerned for my happiness or lack of it. You've done enough already by paying for most of my education." Her horse moved restlessly beneath her, and she steadied both him and herself by reaching out to pat him soothingly on the neck.

Benjamin said, "You know about the trust fund, I take it. How did you find out?"

"Does it matter? I would have preferred to use only what Dad left for me—but there's no use talking about that now. I'm in your debt, Benjamin. Eventually I plan to pay you back."

He sighed, then said, "I meant it for the best, Jacqui. I wanted to do so much more, but Leah—"

Jacqui's defenses slipped back into place. Quietly but firmly she said, "I'd rather we didn't speak of my mother, if you don't mind."

He hesitated, then said, "As you wish. I suppose it's natural for a young woman to want to look ahead to the future, not back. But the past has a way of hanging on to us, all the same. Some time, Jacqui, I wish you'd let me talk to you about what happened back then—just the part that concerns you. It might help you more than you think."

The uneasy feeling in her stomach increased sharply. "No, I'd rather not."

"Well, at least we're talking again. And I'm grateful for that. Have you thought about the fact that you and I are the last members of our family? Surely that's reason enough to maintain some kind of contact? I'd like to be friends with you again, if nothing more."

The sincerity in his voice and the look in his eyes set up conflicting emotions inside her. Looking at him, she felt an awareness of exactly who this man was. He was her uncle; her father's big brother. She could see something of her father in Benjamin's face. The stubborn jaw... the way his brows grew in a thick line above his eyes... *His eyes are different,* she thought, and frowned without knowing it. Benjamin's eyes, though faded now, were the same blue as her father's, but they didn't have that hint of lurking laughter that she remembered so vividly about her father.

Could Mother have loved Benjamin the way she loved Dad? she wondered. *Could she have loved him better?* The tension in her muscles transmitted her uneasiness to the gelding; he danced impatiently, tugging at the reins she held too tightly. Jacqui looked down the trail ahead and saw that Zane and Robert were almost out of sight around the bend.

"I think we'd better just leave things the way they are," she said at last. "I'm sorry, Benjamin. But seeing you just reminds me of things I'd rather forget."

She urged her horse to go ahead, and carried with her the picture of Benjamin's expression. He looked discouraged, weary. Briefly she felt a stab of regret, then shook her head to clear it. It was no good softening toward him; she'd only spoken what was true, what she really felt. If she didn't hold on to old loyalties, what was left for her?

By the end of the day's planned ride, it was obvious that Benjamin had overestimated his strength. He'd insisted on sticking to the scheduled distance, even though he'd been quiet over lunch and looked increasingly fatigued during the day. When they set up camp, Zane saw to it that Benjamin lay down as soon as his tent was ready. When Zane emerged from the tent, he came over to Robert and Jacqui, who were setting up the camp kitchen.

"How's BJ?" Robert asked as Zane approached.

"He claims he only needs some rest. But I think it's a bit more than that."

Jacqui had been watching Zane's face. She saw the depth of his concern, much more than the concern that might be expected of an employee for an employer. She wasn't certain whether her own feelings of concern were on Zane's behalf or due to the compassion she couldn't help feeling toward Benjamin. She'd been rough on him, rejecting his overtures so definitely. But she still couldn't see what else she could have said.

"We carry a radiophone for emergencies," Robert said. "Do you want me to call the Park's rescue service and arrange for transport out of here?"

Zane hesitated, frowning. "I'd like to talk to them later. But BJ is determined to go on with the trek. He's had his medication; it should take effect soon. Jacqui, could we fix him just a light supper?"

"Of course. I have some dry soup I can reconstitute—would that do?" When Zane agreed, she set to work and, improvising a tray from an aluminum container, soon set out a steaming bowl of soup with crackers and a small bowl of cut-up canned fruit.

Zane took the tray in to Benjamin and stayed with him for half an hour. When he came out again, the tight look of worry had eased from his face. "He's going to be all right, at least for now," Zane said as he joined them. "He said thanks for the soup, Jacqui."

Robert got to his feet. "Well, that's good news. But I don't think you'll want to go on to Pine Top Ridge tomorrow, will you?"

Zane shook his head. "I think we should plan on staying here for a day or so, then turn back."

"Okay. I'd better see about hunting up more grazing for the horses. The grass grows a bit thin around here."

After he'd gone, Zane asked, "What happened between you and BJ today, Jacqui?"

Busy at the camp stove preparing dinner for the rest of them, she responded, "What do you mean?"

He came up beside her and waited for her to look up. "You rode together quite a while this morning. Was there anything said that might have upset him?"

She set the skillet down off the fire. "I don't know. Maybe. I told you there could be problems putting us together on a trip like this. In case you're thinking I was rude to him, you're wrong. I told him I knew about the trust fund, and that I intended—"

"I asked you not to mention that to him." Zane spoke sharply.

"It came up." She lifted her chin. "I didn't say I wouldn't mention it to him. Besides, it didn't seem to bother him that I knew. He had to know I'd find out someday. I didn't tell him how I found out, though."

"That's not the point. Jacqui, I've been away from the main office a lot lately. I hadn't realized how sick he was getting until he called me and asked me to return. I'm not sure just how much stress he can handle emotionally."

"Then why on earth did you let him come on this trek?"

"Let him? No one 'lets' BJ do anything. He's his own man, and will be until he dies."

Jacqui watched him as he moved restlessly away a few steps. He ran his hand around the back of his neck, an expression of frustration on his face.

"Zane, you said Benjamin needs an operation to repair his heart valve. Why hasn't he had it done before now? Is it very dangerous?"

"Not as dangerous as it was a few years ago. Techniques in heart surgery have come a long way, but there's no guarantee. So far, he hasn't wanted to take the chance."

"Why not?"

"He's been afraid he might die before he could resolve the situation with you."

"That's not fair," she burst out. "It's not right to put that kind of pressure on me."

Zane came back, stopping in front of her. "It isn't a matter of putting pressure on you. It's just the way the situation is. Can't you see that?"

Feeling numb, she could only shake her head in reply. He went on, "BJ has left you alone all this time just because you wanted it that way. Now he feels that time is running out for him—that this might be his last chance to make amends for the past. He's always loved you, Jacqui. You might ask yourself how you'd feel if you change your mind about him when it's too late to do anything about it."

Tears blurred her vision. She remembered the poignancy in Benjamin's voice when he'd spoken of his friendship with her as a child. But she'd shut him out when he'd asked for a place in her life now. Was it true what Zane had said about her? Was she so unforgiving that she couldn't compromise, couldn't make any concession at all?

She felt a light touch on her cheek, and looked up to see that Zane's eyes had softened. Almost apologetically, he smoothed away a tear from the corner of her eye and smiled wryly. "Poor Sister Wolf. You've had a lot asked of you in a very short time, haven't you?"

Whatever else he might have said was lost when Robert came back to join them. He said, "Zane, you asked me about contacting the ranger station. We can give it a try now, if you like."

The two men went off together, and Jacqui was left alone with her thoughts. As though sensing her troubled state of mind, Buddy remained close at her side during the rest of the evening. Looking into his great golden eyes, she drew what comfort she could in silent communication with a creature she knew gave her a full measure of devotion. *I'm sorry I accused you of abandoning me for Zane, old fellow. I know just how easy it is to fall under his spell.*

Buddy laid his head on her knee and whined a little in his throat. His tail whipped the ground behind him. She smiled. *Yes, you agree with me, don't you? But you like Benjamin, too. I saw him feeding you some of his lunch yesterday.* She scratched behind Buddy's ears, and he closed his eyes blissfully.

Her gaze drifted toward Benjamin's tent. She'd thought of him as her enemy for so long, yet now the thought of him suffering, of the possibility of his dying... Her brow creased in a troubled frown. Of course she didn't want that to happen. But to shoulder the kind of responsibility Zane was talking about...?

She shivered and rubbed her arms to warm them. Zane was asking too much; he wanted even more from her than Benjamin did. But he didn't really know what he was asking. She needed to think—needed to work things out in her head.

It was much later, just before she slipped into her tent for the night, that she searched out her stepbrother and said, "Robert, about tomorrow—"

"Yes, Jacqui?"

"If Benjamin is better, and if we stay around here for a couple of days, I think I might take a side trip to Gramps's cabin."

"By yourself?"

"Yes. You won't need me here, and I'd like to see how the cabin has weathered the past two years."

"All right. But we'd better wait and see what's going to happen with Benjamin. Zane arranged for a private helicopter service to stand by ready to take BJ out by air. But Zane said we couldn't count on your uncle to cooperate if he's not ready to go back yet. He hates having a fuss made over his health, Zane said."

The next morning, Jacqui saw that Zane's evaluation had been accurate. Apparently restored by his medication and the night's rest, Benjamin refused to consider cutting the trip short, much less to go out by helicopter.

"No need to go back yet," he declared with a stubborn light in his eyes. "There's no telling when I'll get a chance for another vacation. I like it here. It'll do me good to laze around for a day or so—maybe get in some fishing. We can talk later about going back."

"Now, BJ," Zane began.

Impatience flashed in Benjamin's eyes. "No, I've made up my mind. I'll be fine if you all just stop fussing. And you can cancel that order for a helicopter, Zane. I'll go out of here the same way I came in, on horseback."

Jacqui, putting away the breakfast things, had to stifle a smile at the look of frustration on Zane's face. Benjamin sounded a lot like she did when she'd made up her mind about something. It sounded as though he could resist just as stubbornly as she, when . . .

The thought broke off and her smile disappeared. No, just because there were surface resemblances didn't have to mean anything special. Genes came down from all your relatives, didn't they?

When Zane reluctantly gave in, she drew in a deep breath and spoke up. "Since you've all decided to stay here today, I'm going to take a short side trip. I have some business to take care of. I need to check out my grandfather's cabin, about five miles east of here. I'll leave Buddy with you, Robert. The trail is likely to be too rough for him."

A moment later, she regretted having mentioned the roughness of the trail. The abrupt silence that followed her announcement quickly erupted into a jangle of protests from everyone except Robert. To her surprise, however, it was Benjamin who objected most strongly.

"It's too dangerous for you to go that far on your own," he said flatly. "You know it's against the guidelines laid out by the Park Service. They say it's best to travel in pairs, at least. Anything could happen! Your horse could stumble on those rocky trails, you could fall and hurt yourself, and with no one near to help you . . . No, it's out of the question for you to go on your own." His color had gone from pale to ruddy. He ran his hand through his hair, ruffling it in his agitation.

"But I'll be perfectly all right," Jacqui said, feeling exasperated, yet somewhat touched in spite of herself. Although his tone was autocratic, his concern was genuine. And valid enough for most people who traveled through the Sawtooths. Speaking reasonably, she said, "I know these mountains like other people know their backyards, Benjamin. I've been on my own up here many times, and nothing bad has ever happened to me."

"But it could happen. Zane, you talk to her."

Zane's gaze was fixed on her, and he was frowning, but he said curtly, "She's made up her mind, BJ. There's nothing we can do to stop Jacqui from going where she wants to go."

"Then you go with her, Zane. There's nothing for you to do around here, anyway. Robert and I will hold down the fort." Benjamin settled back, a relieved smile on his face. As far as he was concerned, he'd come up with the perfect solution.

Jacqui's heartbeat made a quick jump, but Zane spoke before she could protest. "I'm not about to take off for a whole day when you're not well. What if something should happen?"

"Nothing's going to happen. If it will ease your mind, I'll promise not to do anything but rest today. I'll even let Robert call the rangers if I start feeling rocky. Not that it's likely, mind you. I feel just fine. And without you around playing mother hen, I'll be even better."

Jacqui began to regret she'd ever mentioned the trip to the cabin. She moved away to let the men conclude their argument. Obviously Benjamin won, because he was smiling a few minutes later when Zane left him and stalked over to join her.

"That hardheaded, stubborn— What can you do with a man like that?" he grumbled.

"You tell me," she said dryly. She added a filled water canteen to the canvas bag that she was packing with a few provisions.

A reluctant grin formed on Zane's face. "Well, it looks like you're stuck with me for the day, unless you change your mind about going. Or unless you want the argument to start all over again."

"And be responsible for Benjamin having a heart attack on the spot? No, thanks. Grab your gear and let's go saddle the horses."

"Do you mind very much, having me along?" Zane asked a few minutes later, as she was tightening the cinch on the roan gelding.

She glanced over her shoulder at him and was caught up again in the powerful surge of emotions he could stir in her with just a look or a word. What good was the resolution she'd made yesterday to avoid any entanglement with him if she couldn't get a grip on her reactions to him? "No, I don't mind," she replied at last. Her hand fumbled, and the strap slipped, causing the gelding to dance away a little.

Zane came up beside her and laid his hand on the roan's mane, steadying him while she pulled the cinch tight again. In an effort to divert Zane from his intent inspection of her face, she said, "I can see how Benjamin operates in the business world. He tends to walk right over the opposition, doesn't he?"

"He's genuinely concerned about what might happen to you on your own out there, Jacqui. He knows how capable you are, but he's lost every other member of his family—you're all that's left. If he could, he'd wrap you up in cotton to make sure no harm ever came to you. It's a measure of his respect for you that he hasn't tried to do that all these years. But now that he's here with you, he can't hide his feelings so well.''

Jacqui felt a pang of compunction; over the years she'd rejected every overture her uncle had made to her. And just yesterday she'd rejected him again. Yet he still cared enough to worry about her. Gruffly she said, ''Well, I guess it won't hurt to let him have his way in this. It is a good rule not to go off on your own in the wilderness—it's what we tell all our trekkers. I've never thought it applied to me, that's all. Gramps always said your real worth could be measured by how well you could get along with just yourself and nature in the raw.''

''That sounds like a mountain man's philosophy,'' Zane said. ''But you and I both have spent plenty of time alone, Jacqui. What do we have to prove, anymore?''

''Nothing, I suppose.'' She gathered the reins in her hand, ready to mount, then turned suddenly. ''Zane, please don't think that because I'm willing to spend this day with you, that I'm agreeing to anything else. I meant what I said yesterday morning. I'm not ready for an involvement with you.''

A slight smile briefly lit his expression with wry humor. ''I think we're making some progress. 'Not ready' implies that you might be later on. Fortunately, like I said, I'm a patient man.''

Before she could protest that she hadn't meant her words the way he'd taken them, he moved away to mount his own horse.

She thrust her toe into the stirrup, then pulled herself up and over and settled herself in the saddle. Zane reined over to come up close. When he saw her troubled expression, he frowned and said abruptly, "Jacqui, if you'd rather I didn't go with you, just say so. You can take Robert just as well—that should satisfy BJ's notions of safety."

She hesitated, then shook her head. "No, I'd like you to come. I haven't been to Gramps's cabin for two years. It might be easier to have someone along who didn't know him. With Rob, it would be too sad. And I'd like to remember the happier times I spent there."

Zane's frown disappeared, to be replaced by a crooked smile. "That's okay, then. Are you ready to go?"

"Ready," she responded, feeling her heartbeat quicken.

"Have a good time," Benjamin called out as they made a circle around the camp. Buddy barked a farewell, too, and Jacqui and Zane both waved, then rode on. Only Robert was left behind to see the expression of satisfaction that spread across Benjamin's face as the couple broke into a canter and vanished between a gap in the trees that led deeper into the wilderness.

Chapter Seven

It gets rougher farther on," Jacqui called to Zane, who was riding closely behind her on the trail. "But down below there's a dry riverbed that's clear for almost half a mile. I usually let my horse have his head for a gallop there."

"Sounds great to me. Lead on. I'll keep up." She saw the spark of anticipation in his eyes as he grinned at her.

The undergrowth thinned, the rough sloping ground leveled out and they came out into a long, narrow valley. She heard Zane speak softly to his horse at the same time she lowered her reins and nudged the gelding with her heels. Muscles gathered and leaped in response beneath her, and within yards, they were fairly flying over the hard-packed river bottom.

Obstacles were few; Jacqui swerved to avoid a large rock and signaled the gelding to jump a half-buried log. They came down on the other side with a jarring

thump, and she felt her braid begin to unravel. Caught
by the streaming wind, long strands whipped around
her face. She laughed aloud and urged the gelding on
again. It felt glorious to be free, to be running with the
wind, away from the tensions that had made the past
few days so difficult.

The pounding of hooves on her left reminded her
that at least one source of her tensions was still with
her. She threw Zane a glance and saw his teeth flash in
a quick smile. He rode like a cowboy, angling his body
slightly forward against the momentum, holding the
reins in one hand, his thighs and knees doing the main
work of controlling his horse.

Too soon, they reached the end of the long clear
space on the river bottom. With a feeling of regret,
Jacqui reined in just before the level ground petered
out into a rough jumble of rocks and underbrush. She
heard Zane rein in beside her; they'd arrived scarcely
more than a hoofbeat apart. Her breast rose and fell
as she tried to catch her breath. She shook her head to
throw her hair back from her face and exclaimed, "I
think we beat my old speed record for that stretch—
you're a wonderful rider, Zane."

"So are you." He kept his eyes on her face as he
controlled his horse's reluctance to end the gallop.
"Want to go back and do it again?"

She laughed, feeling a spurt of reckless pleasure.
"I'd love to, but I think we'd better save the horse's
strength for the climb up that hill ahead of us."

She turned the gelding and started off at as good a
pace as the trail would allow. She didn't quite trust
herself to linger under the effect of Zane's smile. It
made too much of an inroad on her resolve to keep her
distance from him. *Would it be possible just to be*

friends with him? she wondered. But when she glanced behind and intercepted the look in his eyes, watching her, she jerked her head around again, heat flaring in her cheeks. She knew that friendship was far too lukewarm a word to describe the feelings that were still unresolved between them.

Finally, after half an hour spent picking their way around a rocky gully that led up from the dry riverbed, she pointed ahead and said, "We'll leave the horses about a mile on, near that bluff. We'll have to go the rest of the way on foot."

Zane came up alongside her, his gaze following the direction she'd indicated. "From the condition of the trail so far, I'd say not many people come this way."

She nodded. "There've been several rockfalls since I last came up that hill. The climb used to be easier. Gramps didn't encourage visitors, but he'd tolerate anyone who'd put out the effort to reach the cabin. He usually averaged one or two dozen callers every summer—old hunting and fishing friends, Rob and me, an occasional curious stranger, or some of the Park rangers. We all kept a fairly close eye on him as he got older—packed in supplies for him, that sort of thing."

"How did it happen he could keep a cabin up here? I thought when the Park system took over, private individuals had to move out."

"Gramps's title to his ten acres included lifetime rights to live there, if he chose. He refused to give up the title one minute sooner." She smiled. "I think the government decided it would cause too much bad publicity to try to get him out. Quite a few prominent people had come to think of him as a sort of living museum of the past."

Zane ducked to avoid the scraggy, outreaching limbs of a dead sycamore. "And you stayed up here with him every summer?"

"Mostly, until I started high school. I had less time to come up here, then. Mother needed me more at home. She wasn't very strong the last few years of her life."

They topped a rise and paused to rest the horses for a moment. Jacqui leaned forward to pat the gelding's neck. As though he understood her reluctance to discuss her mother's last illness, Zane asked, "What was it like for you, staying up here?"

She swept her hand out in a wide gesture, taking in the view of pine-topped ridges that undulated toward craggy heights in the distance, and bits of blue lakes that glinted here and there in the rugged scene. "Robert and I had the run of all this territory, as far as you can see. Gramps put no restrictions on where we could go, once he was sure we knew how to take care of ourselves and could find our way back home again."

Zane looked out over the expanse and whistled softly. "That's a lot of freedom to handle. Living in town must have seemed dull after having all this for a playground."

She waited until they moved on before replying. As the horses picked their way through a thick growth of syringa that was just breaking into fragrant bloom, she said, "The change wasn't as difficult as I expected. Anton was beginning to show some of his purebreds about that time, and he kept me busy learning how to ride—the proper way, I mean, for the show ring. I fell in love with horses, and that was my main interest until I started college."

"Do you remember the show you did in San Francisco the year you turned seventeen? I think that was when I realized how fast you were growing up. You put your horse through its paces as cool and steady as if there wasn't an audience of thousands watching you."

She smiled wryly. "Oh, I remember. I was literally growing up then; I'd just added another inch to my height, and I was terribly self-conscious about it. If I looked cool and steady, it was because I was trying to hide how nervous I was." She glanced over at him again and added, "Benjamin told me yesterday that he came to that show, too. You didn't mention he was there when I saw you those few minutes after my ride."

"You were so excited about reaching the semi-finals. I didn't want to say anything to spoil your mood."

"I remember how disappointed I was that you couldn't stay for the party Anton gave me." She decided not to tell him that she'd cried after he left; it had been embarrassing enough when it happened. Her family had thought her tears were due to the over-wrought state of her nerves caused by her excitement at competing in the Grand National.

Now she heard regret in Zane's voice as he said, "BJ and I were scheduled for a hearing in Washington early the next morning, so it was impossible to stay. But I wanted to, very much."

They rode together in silence for a short time until they reached a grassy area surrounded by aspen and fir trees. Jacqui reined in and waited for Zane to do the same. The rocky bluff she'd pointed out earlier loomed on their right. A rivulet of water gurgled not far away. She said, "The horses will be fine here for the time we'll be gone. We can unsaddle and put the gear up in that niche in the bluff.''

They made sure the horses were comfortably settled in the shade of the bluff, munching grass, then they took a short break. Jacqui took the canteen from the backpack, and they each had a drink of the cool, refreshing water.

"I always like to stop here for a while before going on," she said, watching Zane as he tilted his head back for a second drink. "If I haven't been riding much, my legs generally feel rubbery at about this point."

He lowered the canteen and smiled at her as he replaced the cap. "This trip means a lot to you, doesn't it? Coming back to your mountains, I mean."

She was sitting with her back up against a tree, trying to smooth out her tangled hair. "Yes, it does mean a great deal to me. I always feel like I'm coming home when I make this journey to Gramps's cabin."

Zane sat nearby, sharing her shady spot. He leaned back on one elbow, and there was a momentary flash of bleakness in his eyes. "It's been a long time since I felt any sense of homecoming, Jacqui. I envy you." He looked across at her. "I'm glad you're sharing this one with me."

Her heartbeat thrummed in her veins as their gazes held for a long moment. Then he looked away, toward the jagged crests of the distant Sawtooths. She felt a strong pull toward him, a bittersweet yearning. After a moment, she asked, "Zane, don't you have a home of your own someplace?"

His gaze returned to her face. "No. Not the way people usually think of a home. I have apartments in some of the states where TMC maintains regional offices, and I once owned a house in the Lakes region in New York, but that's about it.''

"What happened to the house?"

"I sold it." He'd picked up a stem of pine needles that had broken off from a branch overhead and was twirling it. Now he tossed it onto the ground. "I think I spent a total of about six weeks there in five years. Didn't seem to be much point in keeping it."

She wanted to ask him why he'd bought the house in the first place, but somehow couldn't. Instead she asked, "What about family? You've never mentioned your parents, or any brothers or sisters."

His gaze focused on her. "You've never asked me about my family before."

She picked up the pine twig and plucked absently at the long green needles. They felt sticky, and the pungent scent of the needles rose to her nostrils. "Somehow it never occurred to me to ask, that's all. Or maybe I liked thinking of you as a mystery man. I used to picture you as living such an adventurous life. Every time you dropped in out of the blue, it seemed like my life took a big jump in excitement."

"Would you believe I felt the same way about seeing you?"

"About me?" Her eyes widened. "But my life was so ordinary compared to yours."

His mouth had a whimsical tilt as he made a gesture toward the rocks and trees around them. "Most people would consider your life up here to be very adventurous. I certainly never thought of you as ordinary. The first time I came to see you, it was just another job for BJ. After that—"

He broke off, then shot her a crooked smile. "After that, I started looking forward to the visits. Your attitude toward BJ was hard to take, but I admired your loyalty to your family. I used to wish someone cared about me that much."

Jacqui asked gently, "What about your own family, Zane? You still haven't said anything about them."

"There's not much to say. I can't remember ever seeing my father, and my mother had to abandon me when I was five. I don't know if I have any brothers or sisters."

The matter-of-fact way he stated the bald facts shocked Jacqui. His cool glance didn't invite pity, so she was careful to keep him from seeing how much his words had affected her. "I had no idea, Zane. I'm sorry."

He shrugged. "It could have been worse. The authorities saw to it that I was raised decently enough. But I owe everything else to BJ."

"How do you mean that?"

"For starters, he kept me from going to jail. I belonged to a street gang and got in over my head. BJ was in Detroit on a legal matter for TMC, and he wandered into a courtroom where I was up on an assault charge. He ended up pointing out to the judge that since I'd only just turned eighteen, a bit of leniency might be in order. He offered me a job to get me off the streets, the judge agreed, and I was off the hook."

Jacqui listened in fascination as Zane went on to relate how Benjamin had fed him, given him a short lecture on the necessity of meeting certain standards of honesty and conduct, then had kept him so busy learning the ins and outs of the mining industry that Zane had never looked back.

He concluded, "I managed to get a decent education in between assignments, and BJ kept on giving me as much responsibility as I could handle. I doubt if a real father could have done more for me than BJ has."

Absently Jacqui dropped the pine twig and rubbed her fingers against her jeans to rid them of the clinging needles. "But why would he do all that for you? You were just a stranger to him."

Zane grinned wryly at her. "That was the first thing I asked him that day in Detroit. I was suspicious as hell, at the time. No one had ever offered me anything without strings attached."

"What did he tell you?"

"He said he had a debt he'd promised himself he'd pay if he ever got the chance. He said if anything he did helped me turn around my life, he'd feel like he'd balanced his accounts a little with someone he'd once failed to help."

Jacqui tried to reconcile her impression of Benjamin with the man Zane was describing to her. That her uncle might see the potential in a young man in trouble, and seek to put that potential to work in his own organization was logical enough. It was possible Benjamin might even have guessed the kind of loyalty that might provide a bonus return on his "investment." But to do what he'd done for Zane as a means of canceling out a debt to someone else he'd failed to help? That sounded much too altruistic for the man she knew.

What makes you think you know him? the question slipped past her guard and lodged in her conscience. Could she be so prejudiced against her uncle that she couldn't see any good in him at all? Feeling slightly ashamed of herself, she drew up her knees and hugged them, trying to think. It seemed that so many of her notions were shifting and changing; each day something chipped away at things she'd thought were so certain.

And Zane—she'd never guessed that he might have had an even more traumatic childhood than she'd had. Without Benjamin's intervention would he have gone to the bad? Or would he have overcome the handicaps of his background? Made a success in some other way...

Another pine twig plopped in her lap, tossed there by Zane. She looked up, startled. He smiled and said, "You've become very quiet."

She picked up the twig and drew it through her fingers. "You've given me a lot to think about. I was wondering what would have happened to you if—"

"If BJ hadn't come along? Maybe I'd have made gang leader in another year or so. The turnover was pretty high in that job."

"I don't think so." She released her knees and twisted around to face him. "You're not the criminal type. I can see you as a leader, certainly, and I can see you with a chip on your shoulder, thumbing your nose at a cop, but I can't see you as a criminal."

He grinned at her. "You wouldn't say that if you could have heard the judge in that courtroom. He released me into BJ's custody, but he was pretty pessimistic about my chances of staying on the straight and narrow. But don't stop defending me—I like the idea of you championing my character."

She studied the rugged lines of his face and thought that much of his character was written there. He could be hard at times, as hard as the granite that underlay most of this part of the country. And his eyes could look cool and remote. But those grooves around his mouth sometimes softened, molded into an expression of tenderness; the gray eyes showed intelligence, integrity. Sometimes they warmed, showed deeper fires...

She blinked and dragged her gaze away from his face. Shocked that her own thoughts were leading her into dangerous waters, she scrambled to her feet. "I doubt you need any championing."

He rose swiftly and caught her hand before she could move away. "But I do, Jacqui. Believe me, I do." With scarcely discernible pressure, he gradually pulled her closer, until they were scarcely inches apart.

"No, Zane—please." She felt his thumb near her pulse, and she was afraid her body was betraying her with every beat of her heart. She wanted to moisten her lips with her tongue, but didn't dare.

For a moment that seemed to stretch out forever, they stood face-to-face. His gaze searched hers, as if to see if she really meant what she'd said. Then he nodded and said, "All right, Jacqui."

He released her hand and turned away to scoop up the backpack. She rubbed her fingers in an unconscious effort to stop their tingling, and her shoulders relaxed their tension. She had no reason to feel disappointment, did she? She'd set the limits, and he was abiding by them.

But she knew instinctively that with the emotions that swirled and shimmered in the atmosphere between them, ready to catch fire, it was obvious that it wouldn't take much on the part of either one of them to erase those limits.

She concealed a sigh when he finished settling the light pack into a comfortable position on his back and asked, "How much farther to the cabin?"

"Only another mile, but it's rough going."

"Then we'd better get started."

It took them nearly an hour to traverse the overgrown trail that passed through dense woods, burned-out clearings and occasional rocky outcroppings. Along the way, Jacqui pointed out the various landmarks that marked the path to the cabin. Zane, watching her, observed her increasing tension, and noticed that her eyes were bright with moisture as they neared their goal. *This is hard on her,* he thought. *She's remembering when there was someone waiting to welcome her.*

Finally they crested a hill and paused to survey a narrow strip of cleared land centered by a low, rambling log cabin. An overgrown garden straggled off on one side, and what had once been a pen for animals now leaned derelict on the other side. With an oddly poignant air of dignity, Jacqui gestured widely and said, "This was my grandfather's home, Zane. He built every stick of it himself and lived here for fifty years."

They walked together down the slope to the cabin. When their hands brushed, he caught her hand in his and held it. She looked up at him, gave him a tight smile, then squeezed his hand in silent recognition that his touch was meant to comfort.

"The part added on the left side was the room Gramps built for me. Would you like to see inside?"

Zane nodded, and they mounted the steps of the porch. "These planks are two inches thick," he commented. "And he took the trouble to groove them. They should be pretty well waterproof."

She pulled open the screen door and pushed back the latch which was all that fastened the heavy front door. "He built everything to last. There was some talk of moving the cabin to a museum site, but they gave up the idea—said it would be too difficult to get everything put back together as perfectly as Gramps had made it."

Inside the cabin he was aware of her watching him as he inspected the intricate joinings and carved rafters of the main room. He bent to examine the massive fireplace, then ran his hand over the polished hardwood mantel. She came over to join him and shook her head at the dust that came away on his hand. She pointed up at the empty space over the fireplace. "Gramps hung a sketch here that I drew of him. He was very proud of it. I have it in my room down at Robert's place now."

Zane listened as she went around the various parts of the cabin, explaining this or that device, telling him how she and Robert had packed up many of the innumerable handcrafted items Jim Littlewolf had made; some were in storage as personal keepsakes, others had been donated to a museum in Boise.

"And this is my room," she said at last. "I spent many a night in my bed in that corner, snuggled under the bearskin rug he tanned for me. I used to make up stories to myself, pretending I was an Indian princess living here in splendid isolation, surviving in the wilds of Ed-da-how against all odds."

Zane turned his head and smiled at her. "And did you dream of Indian warriors, brave enough to find the way through to your 'splendid isolation'?"

She blushed, and he knew he'd guessed correctly. She moved toward the window and looked out. "I suppose the isolation will last a little while longer. At least until the Park Service decides to improve the trail up here. Then the trekkers will picnic out where Gramps planted his vegetable garden; they'll fish in his stream and break down the mud walls he built to keep fresh trout available for his larder. Everything will change."

Zane came up behind her and gently rested his hands on her shoulders. He felt the brief tension in her, then felt her relax. "You loved him very much," he said.

She nodded. "He used to say the wilderness was my second school, and he was my schoolteacher. He didn't stint on the lessons he taught, and sometimes the homework was hard. But he gave me some wonderful memories."

She looked over her shoulder at him and smiled. "I'm very glad you came with me today, Zane. At first I thought I wanted to be alone, but somehow it's been better because you're here. I think Gramps would have liked you very much."

Zane had to curb a powerful desire to take her in his arms. Instead he turned her around to face him. Gently he pushed back the hair from her face. She closed her eyes briefly, and he felt a faint tremor pass through her. When she opened her eyes again, it took all his control to hide the depth of his feelings for her.

Jacqui felt a dryness in her throat, and had to moisten her lips before she said, "You're looking at me rather strangely."

"Am I?" He gave her a brief, crooked smile. "I think it's seeing you here—hearing you speak of your life here. I've been getting a much better picture of you, of what made you the woman you are."

"You mean now you see me as a wild mountain woman?" Her smile reached her eyes.

"No, but I see where you get your strength. You've gotten that from the mountains, I think. From the things your grandfather taught you, and from what you found inside yourself up here."

She tipped her head to one side, considering. "Perhaps I have," she agreed.

"You were lucky to have this refuge to come to."

"A refuge? I don't know what you mean."

"A refuge from the past...he unhappiness you felt as a child...whatever memories make you shut BJ out of your life."

She pushed herself away from him and stood in the center of the room. She felt a sharp disappointment that he'd altered the mood between them. "Why are you bringing up those things now?"

"Because this might be the best place for you to look back at them—see why they still have such a hold on you. You're not naturally a hard woman, Jacqui. Yet your view of BJ is so adamant. You don't seem to think logically when it comes to anything having to do with him."

He caught her arm before she could leave the room. "No, don't turn away from it, please, Jacqui. This insistence on not looking back into the past has hurt you badly. Can't you talk about it at all? Is it so bad you can't put it into words?"

Perhaps it was the caring, caressing tone in his voice, or his touch, strong and sure, or the compelling look in his eyes. Or it might have been because they were in her old room in the cabin, her safe place where no one and nothing could harm her. Somewhere deep inside her, something gave way, unlocked. "I can put it into words, yes. If you want to hear them."

His hands smoothed up and down her arms, encouraging her to trust him. "I want to hear. Tell me."

"You're right—this place was a refuge for me. From the gossip... An escape from all the hurtful things I heard people say about my mother and father after he died." The words came out, slowly at first. "It's amazing what adults will say when children can overhear; as though kids won't understand. But I understood well enough."

She shuddered. "They said such terrible things. That my mother was having an affair with Benjamin, that the mine accident was 'awfully convenient,' coming right after Dad and his brother had a big fight."

"Just because people tend to sensationalize a tragedy, that doesn't mean—"

"Oh, I know there wasn't anything to the whispers about the accident. But the way Mother acted about Benjamin..."

Her voice trailed off. Zane tipped up her chin and asked, "You thought there might be some truth in the other things they said about your mother and BJ?"

She nodded slowly, for the first time admitting to another person the fear that had been buried inside her so long. "After Dad's death, Mother just sort of drew in on herself. She was still kind and sweet, but so many times I felt like she just... wasn't there for me. After she married Anton, I thought she'd change, but she was never really the same as when Dad was alive.

"I told myself that the reason she'd never talk about Benjamin was because she hated him. But it could have been that she just felt guilty for loving him instead of Dad. You know she asked for Benjamin to come to see her when she was dying—you were there."

She rubbed her arms as if cold; Zane drew her down to sit on the hand-hewn planks that formed a window seat. Clasping her hands in his, he said, "Even if what you say is true, it's their tragedy, Jacqui, not yours. You can't let it haunt you now."

She shivered and looked down. "But it does haunt me, if I let myself think about it, because—"

"Because what?"

"Because I'm not sure Benjamin isn't my father."

He must have stared at her for a full ten seconds. "You must have some reason for thinking he might be."

"Oh, there's nothing concrete—intuition, instinct—the way Mother acted whenever his name was mentioned. She used to look at me sometimes so sadly, as if she regretted something terribly, and it involved me."

Jacqui jumped up and began pacing the floor by the window seat. Zane watched her, his brow creased in a concerned frown. She jammed her hands into the back pockets of her jeans and said, "So now you know the reason I've tried to shut it all out—I don't really want to know for sure. I loved Dad—I thought Mother loved him, too. If it's true, if Mother did betray Dad..."

She stopped pacing and spread out both hands in a supplicating gesture. "I just can't think of her that way. I can't!"

"So every time BJ tried to get near you..."

"I couldn't let him get close. These past few days I've felt so terribly disloyal to Dad—to my mother's memory."

Swiftly Zane came out of the window seat and caught her hands in his. "Damn those evil-minded, loose-tongued gossips! You've held it all inside you all these years. Didn't your mother realize what was going on? Why didn't she straighten things out? Or your grandfather?"

"They were trying to protect me—"

His arms went around her. "From what? What could be worse for a young girl than not knowing what to believe?"

"It wasn't their way to talk about such personal things. Maybe it was the Shoshone way—"

He groaned and buried his face in her hair; his hands stroked over her shoulders and down her back. "And so you became little Sister Wolf, fighting your own devils all by yourself. Oh, Jacqui, my love . . . my own love . . ."

He tipped her face up and began to kiss her; his lips touched her brow, her cheeks, brushed across her lips. His tenderness was like the sunshine that poured in through the uncurtained window to bathe them in light. Never had she felt such closeness . . . such belonging . . . And then his arms tightened around her, and she reached around him in turn. It felt so right— so wonderful—like coming home.

Home is Zane. The realization seemed to flash through her whole being, along with his words. *My love,* he'd called her.

"Zane?"

He was pressing kisses on her throat now; the sensations he created in her made her catch her breath. "Yes, Jacqui?"

"You called me your love."

"Yes. Because you are my love. From the first day I met you."

"It shouldn't be possible—if you added together all the hours we've ever spent together, it would only be—"

"It would only be a beginning, you mean." His mouth was now exploring the tender, sensitive skin down the side of her neck. "We've wasted so much time...so many years when we could have been together."

His lips on her skin created shivers of delight that washed over her. She was aware of his body against hers, hard and strong, and of the tender, caressing movements of his hands on her hair, her shoulders, the pliant curve of her back as she swayed against him. She felt tears sting her eyes.

"When you hold me like this, I forget everything else. How can I trust my own judgment?" Her voice was husky.

"Forget the questions. Just let yourself feel, Jacqui. Feel the magic."

He drew her down into the window seat again, nestling her close in his lap with his arms strong around her. She slid her arms around his neck, lifting her face for the kiss that hovered a breath away from her lips. A sound like a sob escaped her throat as his mouth covered hers once more and her arms tightened around him. Her senses spiraled away from her in a dizzy dance of rising joy. She felt as though she were one with him and the sunlight that streamed through the window like a benediction.

Chapter Eight

Buddy came out to greet Zane and Jacqui as they neared the camp at early twilight. He rushed through the row of trees bordering the campsite to prance around the horses, his tail wagging and his tongue hanging out in a doggy smile.

Jacqui dismounted and bent over to pat him, scratching him behind his ears with her two hands. "You act as though we've been gone a week, not just a day."

She glanced up at Zane, still feeling the glow of the past few hours with him. The day might have been a year, as far as she was concerned, and still it wouldn't have been long enough to contain the joy she felt spilling over inside. From Zane's expression as he returned her smile, she knew he felt the same way.

It wouldn't be easy to shake off the spell of all that had happened at Gramps's cabin that afternoon. Jacqui had taken Zane to see some of the special places of her childhood; the tree house aerie she'd helped build, the plank bridge over the stream where the fish farm had been and the rambling enclosures where her grandfather had provided housing for the small wild creatures she used to bring back to the cabin for "study."

Zane had been eager to know everything about her and had peppered her with questions. He'd touched her at the slightest excuse, helping her cross the smallest obstacle in their path. Often they simply stopped and kissed, giving way to the delight they found in the day and in each other.

Now they left the horses to graze with the others and walked side by side back to the campsite. Jacqui sighed. Their private time together was over. *At least for now,* she amended, trying to tamp down the feelings of joy bubbling up inside her.

Benjamin rose to his feet when he saw them. "I thought I heard the horses coming back. How did your day go?" He looked keenly at both of them, then smiled broadly.

Zane grinned back at him. "It was great. How about you—how are you feeling?"

Benjamin waved his hand in a dismissing gesture. "I told you I'd do just fine once everybody quit fussing. Do you see those trout Robert's getting ready to cook over there? I caught half of them."

They went over to the camp stove, where Robert lifted his stirring spoon in a mock salute. A dish full of cleaned trout dredged in flour awaited frying in a large iron skillet and a pot of beans simmered on the front burner. An appetizing smell of corn bread came from the Dutch oven. Robert said, "You're back just in time. I'll wait till you finish washing up before I start cooking the trout."

Jacqui reached for a spoon and scooped up some beans. "Um, that's good—you put barbecue sauce in, hmm?"

He took the spoon away from her, chiding, "Hey, wait till everything's ready. It's a good thing I fixed plenty. You two look hungry."

"We missed lunch," Zane explained as he bent over the pot and sniffed the tangy fragrance. "I accidentally dropped the backpack in the stream behind the cabin, and our sandwiches got soaked."

He looked over at Jacqui, and she saw the laughter in his eyes. She couldn't help grinning back, but she was conscious of Robert's raised eyebrows. She wasn't about to tell him that the reason the backpack had fallen into the stream was that they'd stopped to kiss on the narrow footbridge. When they finally did think about eating, they'd discovered the pack lodged against some rocks fifty yards down the stream.

"We didn't go completely hungry," she said to Benjamin, who was standing nearby, his eyes alive with interest. "We looked around Gramps's garden and found a big Hubbard squash that survived the winter—it must have been two feet long and was hard as a board. Zane chopped it up with an axe, and we roasted the pieces in the fireplace, pioneer style."

Zane smiled at her again, and for a moment it was as though they were back in the cabin, sitting on the floor in front of the fireplace, laughing as they fed each other smoky pieces of yellow squash.

Benjamin chuckled, but Robert cleared his throat and rattled the skillet on the stove. "Uh, if you two will give me some room here, I can get on with fixing supper."

He sounded disgruntled. Jacqui gave him a quick look and responded, "Okay, Rob. I'll only need a few minutes to wash up and change." To Zane she said, "You won't want to take any longer, either, considering the water temperature in the 'washrooms' up here. Take your pick—upstream or downstream? I'll go the other way."

His eyes told her he'd just as soon share either direction with her, but with Benjamin and Robert watching them, he only smiled and said, "I'll take downstream."

"Ten minutes, Jacqui, if you want any of these trout," Robert called after her as she hurried toward her tent. "BJ and I worked up quite an appetite ourselves."

She grabbed some fresh clothes and a towel and headed upstream, telling Buddy to stay behind. It was not quite dark yet; she was able to find a deep enough spot in the broad stream that rushed down from the hills and curved around the campsite.

From a distance downstream, she heard a shout of surprise from Zane and grinned. More accustomed to the wilderness style of bathing, she stripped quickly and waded in. She gasped at the cold, then lowered herself completely into the water, being careful to keep her hair dry. Goose bumps covered her arms and legs as she washed herself thoroughly. In a few minutes she was back on the bank, rubbing her naked body with the rough towel.

A stray breeze passed by, lifting the hairs at her nape, and suddenly she didn't feel at all cold. Her skin tingled in remembrance of Zane's breath touching her

there, and on her throat . . . His hands touching her
breasts . . . A wave of heat washed over her and she
stood motionless, clutching the towel. They'd come
very close to making love completely, but hadn't. Zane
had drawn back, then had held her tightly while the
aching need he'd created inside her had gradually
calmed, subsided. *Did he know, somehow, that I'm a
virgin? Was that why he held back?*

Something splashed out in the water, and she
blinked back into the present. *I should dunk myself in
the stream again,* she thought with wry humor. If she
didn't cool down everyone would guess what was
happening, and it would be nice to keep the magic between just the two of them a little longer.

By her reckoning, she was only a minute or so over
the limit Robert had set when she returned to camp.
Zane appeared a few minutes later, his hair still damp.
He grinned at her, and she grinned back. Suddenly it
didn't seem to matter that their feelings must be obvious to everyone, even Buddy, who couldn't make up
his mind which one of them to devote his attention to.
*It would be hard to miss that things are different be-
tween us now,* she thought, *the way Zane keeps looking at me like I was the prize he just won at the fair.
And I can't seem to stop smiling at him.*

Dinner was a festive meal. Jacqui thought that never
had a gathering been so congenial, as stories and conversation flew back and forth. She ate the delicious
food and listened to the other three talking about Jim
Littlewolf's cabin and the artifacts remaining there.
She kept losing the thread of the discussion, however,
because her mind kept running over a replay of the
events of her day with Zane. *I do love him and he loves
me, I know he does,* she repeated wonderingly to her-

self, testing the words in her mind. She didn't try to
stop the tremulous joy that kept springing up inside
her, testing the boundaries of her new happiness.
Maybe, somehow, it would work out for them...

She complimented Benjamin on the trout. "I'm
glad you felt up to fishing today. Fresh trout is always
a treat, especially on the first trek of the season."

He beamed at her. "Fishing relaxes me, it's a great
sport. I'd like to do some more tomorrow."

"Would you really like to stay another day, BJ?"
Zane gave him a thorough scrutiny, as though searching out signs of illness or weariness. "We could start
the journey back tomorrow. We'll need to travel in
easy stages, if you insist on going out on horseback
again."

"I'm having the time of my life. Another day of
fishing will do me a lot more good than a tub full of
medicine. How about the rest of you?"

Robert spoke up. "I could take a couple of the
horses and do some repair work on the trail to Pine
Top Ridge. I spotted two fallen trees, and there might
be more farther along."

"I could give you a hand," Zane offered. "A job
like that would be easier with two men."

Robert hesitated, and Jacqui caught Zane's fixed
gaze on her. *He wants me to have the chance to spend
some time with Benjamin,* she thought. Among the
many things they'd discussed on the ride back to camp
was her need to try to put to rest some of her questions about Benjamin. So when Robert glanced over
at her to see how she felt about Zane's suggestion, she
said, "You should take Zane up on that offer, Rob.
While you're gone, I might get in a little fishing my-

self with BJ. Maybe we can catch enough trout for another feast tomorrow night."

"That will be fine, Jacqui. I'd enjoy your company very much." Benjamin's face lit up with pleasure.

"Then it's all settled." Zane clapped his hands on his knees and pushed himself up from his seated position on a log. "Jacqui, how about taking an after-dinner stroll with me? I need to work off some of that great food."

Robert frowned, and Benjamin smiled benignly. Jacqui picked up an extra sweater and they left the camp, taking the downstream path.

Content to walk along hand in hand, they didn't speak at first. During supper the last of the twilight had faded, but now the moon spread light everywhere. Their path led to a broad, smooth outcropping of granite, and they walked out on it until they reached the end that jutted out over the stream. About ten feet below was a wide, deep pool. The moon, reflected in the pool, seemed to be sailing serenely in two skies.

"It's beautiful here, isn't it?" she asked dreamily, and leaned against him when he put his arm around her waist.

"I'd think that stream was more beautiful if it hadn't turned me blue when I took my bath a while ago."

She smiled. "I know; I heard you yell. But you must be tough to go all the way in. You came back to camp with your head wet. At least I had enough sense to keep my hair dry."

His laugh came low and thrilling. As naturally as breathing, his arms encircled her and he drew her snugly up against his body. "The only problem with your romantic moonlit evenings up here is the fact that you have to bundle up so much. How many sweaters do you have on right now?''

She slid her hands beneath his windbreaker and hugged him. It felt wonderful to be able to laugh with him. "Only three, if you don't count my wool camisole."

"Wool camisole? What's that?"

She locked her hands behind his back and tilted back her head. "An intimate garment designed for comfort and warmth, as if you didn't know."

"I'm not as well versed in feminine garments as you seem to think." His hands had found their way through layers of clothing and now smoothed up over the one garment remaining between his hand and her skin. "Ah, I see. You're right. It does feel comfortable and warm."

She laughed breathlessly as his exploring hands brushed lightly over her breasts. "It wasn't designed with your comfort in mind, just mine."

He sensed the shyness she still felt at his intimate touch; his hands spread out on her back, and he pressed her close. His tone changed, dropped, as he said huskily, "Jacqui, you do feel so good to me. You *are* good for me. I can't bear to think of how we might have missed each other. If BJ hadn't called me back when he did..." He shook his head. "I've often thought of coming to Idaho to look you up again, but I might not have done it."

Remembering how she'd rejected all of his attempts to see her, six years before, she said, "I understand."

"I hope so. I feel like a kid in a candy store tonight. It seems like I've been alone so much of my life.

First I was scrambling to stay alive in Detroit, then working my head off trying to make BJ feel like he'd backed the right man. When I made those quick stops to see you, I was usually on my way to some isolated spot where I'd be working twenty hours a day for weeks at a time. It wasn't always easy to pull myself away and leave you."

She brought her hands around to rest on his chest, gently caressing the warm, hard muscles she could feel beneath her fingers. She guessed that not all of his long working hours had been spent at desks; he must have spent a lot of time using those muscles one way or another in the course of his field work. "I never saw how lonely it might be for you," she mused aloud. "I don't know why I assumed your life was just one glamorous adventure after another."

His lips brushed the side of her neck below her ear. "There might be about ten percent glamour and adventure. The rest is just hard work, mixed in with some very tedious waiting in airports all over the world."

He lifted his head, and she reached up to frame his face with her hands. "Zane, darling, I wish I'd known. I was a thoughtless teenager. I didn't think about how difficult it might be for you to fit those visits into your schedule."

"Those visits to you gave me a center, Jacqui," he said huskily, and the moonlight showed her his eyes glittering with strong emotion. "A center I used to look forward to coming back to, even though it took me a while to realize why it was so important to me. When things came to an end six years ago, I felt like a hole had been carved out of the middle of my life. It's been empty ever since, until now."

"Oh, Zane," she said, her voice breaking a little. In comparison with him, she'd had so much—her family, Marybeth and her friends at school.

"So now you know why I feel like a kid in a candy store tonight," he said.

She buried her face against him and they clung tightly to each other for a long, wordless moment. Finally, his voice sounding uneven, he said, "I think we'd better head back. I'm running out of self-control."

The camp was dark and quiet when they returned; Benjamin and Robert had already gone to their tents. Zane stopped her just as she was about to lift the flap of her tent. In a low tone, he said, "Jacqui, before you go in, I want to say thanks."

"For what, Zane?" She looked up at him and thought how the nighttime suited him. His curling dark hair caught the gleam of moonlight, and his shadowed features had a mystery about them that made her heart pound.

"You made BJ's day for him. He was thrilled that you volunteered to spend some time with him tomorrow."

A troubled frown creased her forehead. "I wish it didn't mean so much to him, Zane. If he wants more from me than I can give, I'm afraid it will just make things worse in the end."

"Don't worry about it. Just see what happens. I'm sure it will all work out." He reached out and touched the side of her neck beneath her flowing hair. Catching up a handful, he rubbed the silken strands gently between his fingers. "I can hardly let you go tonight. Have I told you how beautiful you are?"

"Mmm, you're very good for my ego." She tried to respond lightly, but the warm tone in his voice touched her deeply.

His hand slid around to the back of her neck. "You're good for me in every way. All I have to do is see you, or hear your voice, to want to touch you, to hold you in my arms and kiss you the way we did this afternoon in the cabin."

In unconscious reaction to his suddenly deeper tone, the tip of her tongue came out and ran over her lips to moisten their dryness. "At the moment, I don't think that would be such a good idea. Rob and Benjamin have seen enough already to have a pretty clear picture that something is happening between us."

"Do you mind them knowing?" His fingers stroked her nape, moving with a slow touch that made her melt inside.

"It's just a little embarrassing," she admitted. "I told Rob before we started on the trek that you were the last man I'd ever get involved with."

She saw the flash of Zane's teeth as he smiled. His hand drew her closer. "Then you had it right. I want to be the last man you'll ever be involved with. This is serious for me, Jacqui. I've never felt this way about a woman before."

Through the lump in her throat, she said huskily, "Me, too. I didn't know I could feel the way I do when you kiss me. This afternoon I almost didn't want you to stop."

"Believe me, it wasn't easy to stop. I wanted to make love to you—wanted to claim you so there could be no turning back, for either of us."

"Then why—"

He kissed her on the forehead. "If I didn't care so much about you... But you'd had enough to deal with already. You were keyed up, vulnerable. When we do make love, I want it to be when it's only because of the way we feel about each other. You're worth waiting for, Jacqui. I want to take the time for things to be right between us."

With her heart almost too full for words, she lifted herself up on tiptoe and kissed him. "You make me believe things will be right... Thank you, darling, for being the man you are. So I'll say good night, for now." She pulled herself out of his arms and slipped into her tent.

From the darkness outside, she heard him say softly, "Good night, love. Sleep well." And then he strode away.

The next morning Jacqui woke up with a nameless feeling of dread. It was a moment before she pinpointed the reason, then she remembered. She'd committed herself to spending the morning alone with Benjamin. The thought was enough to make her apprehensive through all the morning routine. Even Zane's encouraging smile just before he left with Robert didn't help very much. "Are you sure you don't want us to take Buddy?" he asked her. "He might get in the way of your fishing."

"He knows how to behave. Zane, I—"

Taking advantage of the fact that Benjamin and Robert weren't looking, Zane gave her a swift kiss on the mouth. "Don't worry—you'll get along fine with BJ. I've survived all these years with him, haven't I?"

She didn't smile back. "He's a tycoon. He can make a business decision and cause stocks to tumble on Wall

Street. I've seen pictures in the paper of him with the President. What do I have in common with a man like that?"

"Take another look at him; he's only a man with good points and bad points like all the rest of us." Zane caught her clenched hand and gently opened her fingers. "Talk to him, let him help you understand what happened between him and your parents. Knowing the truth will make all the difference in the world, I'm sure."

"I admit I feel better toward him since I've learned what he did for you. But I'm a little afraid he might just try to take me over, like he did my parents." She avoided putting into words the deeper fear she'd revealed to him already.

"I think you'll find a lot in him to like," Zane said encouragingly. "From what you've told me about your grandfather, I think the two of them had a great deal in common. BJ has the same independent spirit, and he's been a pioneer, too, in his way."

Their conversation broke off when Benjamin, wearing his fishing gear, came over to them. Shortly thereafter, Zane and Robert took their leave, and she was left facing Benjamin. He smiled genially and hefted his fishing pole. "Well, I'm ready when you are. I'm really looking forward to this, Jacqui."

She chose the easiest route upstream to the fishing spot she had in mind. Benjamin seemed to be in no hurry to discuss any sensitive matter, and gradually she relaxed.

They came to a place where the stream widened out, offering room to cast their lines. "This is a good place," she said. "The sun has warmed the water, and the trout will be more interested in your flies. But watch out for drop-offs. The bottom is a bit uneven.''

Since she had no wading boots, Jacqui fished from the bank. Buddy watched alertly from the shade of a clump of aspen trees. With the rapt concentration of a dedicated fisherman, Benjamin waded slowly out to midstream, casting his line ahead of him, then slowly reeling in the line to do the same thing all over again.

His movements were rhythmical, soothing. She watched him, pondering on the best way to broach the questions that bothered her. Her mouth twisted wryly. She'd made such an issue of not wanting to speak of the past, and now she was trying to figure out the best opening to the subject. It seemed as though Benjamin had made up his mind not to press her anymore. So it was going to be up to her.

The grass was lush where she was sitting, and she settled back and yawned. It wouldn't hurt to rest for a short while, then talk later when Benjamin had had his fill of fishing. Last night she hadn't slept as much or as deeply as she probably needed. She'd had so many absorbing things to think about...the way Zane had looked at her when he'd said goodnight...the way his lips had felt when she kissed him...

In a pleasant state of lethargy, she drifted off into a daydream. Downstream she heard the bubbling murmur of the water as it ran more rapidly over rocks. Where they were, there was only the sound of the breeze in the fir and aspen, and the occasional plop of Benjamin's lure in the water. Her own rod dangled down at the tip as her hand gradually relaxed.

"Aha!" Benjamin's triumphant shout brought her head up with a jerk. He had a strike. She watched him move out deeper, heedless that the water was close to the top of his wading boots. His arms were extended, and she recognized the same intensity of purpose she'd seen in him that day near Sun Valley. He was the picture of a man determined to win.

"Be careful," she called. "There's a deep hole not far from where you're standing."

"I've got him," he cried confidently. "It's a three-pounder, at least. Come on, fella, just a little more to the right—"

Jacqui set her rod down and jumped to her feet. Benjamin staggered, but he didn't loosen his grip on his rod. *Oh, Lord, his heart!* She began kicking off her boots.

She waded out into the stream and caught him around the waist just as he slipped and started to lose his balance. "Come back, Benjamin," she said breathlessly. "You're going out too far."

He was reeling in as fast as he could. "I've got him, I tell you! No, there he goes again. Hang on, Jacqui, don't let go!"

She hung on to him with all her strength while he maneuvered frantically to keep the trout from escaping into a tangle of roots on the far side of the stream. Her bare foot slipped on a rock beneath the water and they almost went under. *Enough is enough,* she thought, then leaned backward and heaved.

The chief executive officer of TMC, tycoon and friend of presidents, came protesting—but he came—letting her guide him backward until they reached their side of the bank and the shallows. "We got him! Isn't he a beauty? Where's the damned net? Would you get the net, Jacqui?"

Soaked from her heels to her waist, Jacqui silently did as he asked, and soon the trout was safely landed.

Benjamin was breathing hard, but his face was exultant. Two bright spots of red marked his cheeks, and his white hair stood up in a tangled fluff around his head. He beamed at Jacqui, then his face fell, ludicrously. "Oh, my God, Jacqui—what did I do to you?"

"I'm all right." She lifted one leg and shook it to dislodge a clump of leaves from her wet jeans. "Why on earth didn't you just let him go?"

"I couldn't let him get away—not a fish of that size! I—" He caught himself, then looked at her with a sheepish smile. "Oh, hell, Jacqui, I just didn't think. It was stupid of me. I'm sorry."

Jacqui went behind some bushes and took off her jeans to wring them out. Her blouse wasn't that wet and would dry quickly. She tugged the jeans back on, then went to put on her boots.

"Don't worry," she said brusquely. "The sun's out and it's plenty warm. There's no need to rush back to camp. I'll dry out in no time. It isn't the first time I've taken an unexpected dip in a trout stream."

Benjamin sat down on a large rock and stared at her unhappily. "It's all my fault. I never can seem to do things right where the people I care about are concerned. And I wanted things to be right this time. Can you forgive me?" He leaned toward her, anxiety showing in his face as he waited for her reply.

She met his gaze and knew he was apologizing for more than the soaking she'd just received. She must have hesitated a fraction too long, because his shoulders slumped, and he said heavily, "You have a lot to forgive me for, I know." His hand shook slightly as he rubbed it across his eyes. "I wanted so much to have a chance to talk to you—to try to break down the wall that's been between us."

Buddy had been an interested spectator in all that had been happening; he came up to Jacqui and lay down beside her, as though he sensed the turmoil of her thoughts. She reached for him now, seeking comfort in the familiar feel of his thick warm coat. Stroking him also gave her an excuse to keep her head down for a moment. When she had her expression under control again, she looked up and said, "I'm ready to listen if you want to talk to me, Benjamin."

He took a deep breath. Relief showed on his face as he braced his hands on his knees and said, "Thank God. You don't know how difficult it's been guarding my tongue around you these past few days. I hoped... Well, never mind what I hoped. It's as painful for me as it must be for you, raking up the past."

"That's why I wanted to avoid it." Her voice was low, and he nodded before he went on.

"After the accident that took your father, Jacqui, I waited a long time, thinking you were too young to understand about that quarrel you heard between us. And then later, I couldn't get through to you at all to explain." He paused, then said, "Can you trust my word enough to accept my version of what happened, Jacqui? There isn't anyone alive now to verify it."

Their eyes met for a long moment. Then she nodded. "I'll trust you. Because I think you're too proud a man to lie when your word is at stake."

She saw the release of tension around his eyes. He smiled at her. "You have so much of your mother in you, Jacqui, and perhaps even more of me."

A chill passed over her, and she wrapped her arms protectively around her middle. Painfully she said, "Benjamin, if you're going to tell me that it was true, what was said about you and mother—" She broke off, unable to continue.

Benjamin looked horrified as he grasped her meaning. "No, no—it was never like that between your mother and me. The gossip you heard was only that, gossip. People will always put the worst interpretation on any affair where two men and a woman are involved. I meant that because you're a Treherne; we have the same blood in us, you and I. I'm not your father, Jacqui."

Profound relief flooded through her, making her feel almost giddy. She swallowed to ease her dry throat and relaxed her tense posture. Tentatively she said, "There must have been something between you. Mother asked for you when she was dying. And you arrived in your jet—just in time." Jacqui's throat felt tight. How vivid that memory still was to her.

"I loved her. That much was true." He passed his hand over his eyes again. "God, I knew this was going to be hard, but I didn't know how hard. The fact is that I fell in love with Leah the first time I saw her, just after she got engaged to my brother. There was nothing I could do about the way I felt, and I didn't even try. But later, after you were born, I saw how he treated her, and I tried my best to help."

"What do you mean how he treated her?" Jacqui stiffened again, defensively. "They were happy together—I used to hear her singing. Dad could always make her laugh, even when she was sad."

Benjamin's smile twisted. "I said I wouldn't lie to you. And you remember right. Johnny was a likable

fellow; always ready with a fast quip and the look of
the devil in his eyes. Maybe that's why Leah loved him
instead of me—women seem to like that kind of thing.
I never could fathom it.''

Benjamin looked up again, his expression regret-
ful. ''But the bottom line was that Johnny caused
Leah a lot of grief, too, especially after you came
along and she wasn't able to flit off with him every
time he took a notion to try something new.

''I tried to get him interested in the mine, hoping
he'd settle down. He'd learned demolition in the Navy,
and for a while he seemed to like his job. I started
hoping we might eventually become partners. But
most of all, I wanted you and your mother to have
some stability in your lives—with me there to look after you when Johnny couldn't or wouldn't.''

Jacqui heard the echo of pain in his voice and
waited for him to go on. Buddy whined a little, and
she relaxed the grip she had on his fur.

''The quarrel you heard that day,'' Benjamin said,
''came about because Johnny told me he was quitting
and taking Leah and you to Alaska on some fool hunt
for a gold mine. I lost my temper . . . I'm not sure now
what all I said, but I was rough on him.''

Jacqui broke in. ''You said you'd rather see him
dead than to go on treating Mother the way he had
been. I remember you raised your fists as though you
wanted to hit him.''

''Maybe it would have been better if we'd fought
with our fists. It might have settled something then.
Instead I insisted he stay to finish blasting the new
section of mine the next day. I was trying to buy time,
hoping he'd change his mind about leaving. I couldn't
bear to lose Leah—or you. I loved you like the

daughter I knew I'd never have. Instead I lost everything. And Johnny lost his life."

He rested his head on his hand and sighed. Jacqui was amazed to hear herself say, "It was an accident. The fuses were faulty."

"I know. But I heard the gossip that said he was careless that day because of our quarrel. On my word of honor, Jacqui, I don't believe that was true. Johnny never was one to hold a grudge. I think he was just in a hurry to get the job done. And so he took one too many shortcuts and paid for the last one with his life."

There was a long silence. Then Jacqui drew in her breath. "Why didn't Mother want to see you after Dad's funeral? I know she burned some letters you sent. And she never wanted to talk about you, or about what happened."

Benjamin, sitting hunched over, shook his head. "I'm not sure I can answer that. I remember you'd get terribly upset when I came to the house; and in a small town it was impossible to see Leah anywhere else. The gossip was bad enough already. I think that's what broke her spirit. She was proud, for all her gentle ways. So in the end, I helped her in the only way I could—by staying away and letting her rebuild her life in her own way. She married Anton Janek two years later."

Jacqui, with her own newly found love, sensed just what that decision to stay away must have cost her uncle. *Poor Benjamin,* she thought. *He tried to arrange my parents' lives for the better and only succeeded in ruining his own chances for happiness, as well as theirs.* After what had happened, it was easy to guess why he'd never married. As for Leah, whatever she'd felt for Benjamin, it had undoubtedly been eas-

ier for her to just withdraw from the problem and lock
it away in the past.

Like I've been doing, Jacqui thought with a sudden flash of insight. Robert was right—it would have
been better if she'd faced the past a long time ago.
She'd have saved herself a great deal of unhappiness.
Frowning, she studied Benjamin, who was lost in some
inner vision of his own. His expression was sad, but it
was a resigned sadness; he'd carried it for many years,
and for him there would be no regaining what he'd
lost.

Aloud, she said, "It was my father you meant when
you told Zane about the debt you felt you owed
somebody, wasn't it? He was the reason you helped
Zane."

Benjamin looked at her. "Zane told you about that?
Yes, it was Johnny I wanted to help and couldn't."

She felt a wave of pity and sadness. It had all gone
wrong for Benjamin. And by her determined rejec-
tion of him, she'd cut her uncle off from his one remaining link to his brother and the woman he'd loved.

But I don't think I'd have believed him before now,
she thought with a sense of discovery. *Not until I
found out for myself what it is to care for someone
that deeply.* She felt a rush of gratitude toward Zane
for helping her open her eyes and rid herself of her old
fears.

Compassion filled her heart, and the love she felt
for Zane spilled out to include her uncle. She reached
out and touched his arm. When he looked up at her,
she smiled at him and said, "I'm glad you told me
about this, BJ. You've helped me resolve some things
I've struggled with for a long time. I hope it's not too
late for us to become friends?"

A vast relief showed in his eyes. He clasped her hand in both of his and gripped her fingers tightly. "Jacqui, that would make me so happy, you wouldn't believe—" Emotion choked his voice. Then he said, "I wish I could see Leah just once more—to tell her how much she has to be proud of in you."

"Thank you, BJ." Tears sparkled in her eyes as she smiled rather shakily at him. "Before I make myself wet all over again by crying, why don't we go back to our fishing instead? We have some time to make up in getting to know each other. What do you say? Deal?"

His eyes were misty, too. He held out his hand and said, "Deal. Shake on it?"

They shook hands solemnly while Buddy looked on, panting, seeming to smile in approval.

Chapter Nine

The first thing Zane heard on returning to camp that afternoon was the sound of Jacqui's laughter. The clear musical sound brought a smile to his own lips at the same time it eased the tight feeling in his chest. He increased his pace, and seconds later reached the clearing.

Benjamin, wearing a large apron, was seated on a low tree stump with a bucket on the ground between his knees. He had a knife in one hand and a slippery fish in the other. The fish had a smear of dirt and dry leaves down one side. Jacqui, standing nearby with her hands on her hips, was shaking her head at him.

"BJ, the idea is to clean the fish, not to teach them to walk on land. You have to hang on to them."

He grinned as he looked up at her. "They're not built to hang on to. Are you sure you don't want to take over here? No one ever made me do the cleaning before."

"Then it's about time you learned. You—" Some sound Zane made caused her to look in his direction. He saw her face light up; her dazzling smile of welcome jolted him in his midsection. She called out, "Hi! We were wondering when you two were going to get back."

He reached her and had to make a physical effort to keep from taking her into his arms. Her extraordinary eyes were wide and luminous, and a faint pink flush appeared in her cheeks as he continued staring at her. But she stood her ground, and he sensed that she, too, was imagining his arms around her, and his lips joining with hers in the kiss they both wanted.

Behind him he heard Benjamin clear his throat. Zane looked away from Jacqui and belatedly said, "Hello, BJ. No need to ask if you had a successful morning. That's quite a catch you have there."

"I could say the same for both of you." The twinkle in Benjamin's eyes showed satisfaction as well as approval. "I may be speaking prematurely, but I'd like to say that I couldn't be happier."

A glance at Jacqui's face told Zane that she had mixed feelings about this frank comment on their new relationship, but before either of them could respond, Robert joined them in the clearing. His expression as his glance fell on the two of them standing so close together wasn't nearly as approving as Benjamin's. *I'm going to have to have a talk with Rob,* Zane thought. *And fairly soon.*

The only moment Zane had for a private conversation with Jacqui came while Robert and Benjamin were filling their plates at the camp stove. He drew her to one side and said softly, "I'd say your morning with BJ was a great success, judging by the grin on his face.

I haven't seen him looking so well and happy in years.
How about you?''

She tilted her head to one side and regarded him
with a wry smile. "It wasn't as difficult as I thought it
would be. BJ is quite an interesting person, if a bit
overpowering at times.''

He decided that although she'd come a long way,
she still had some reservations about her uncle.
"And?" His eyes searched hers.

Her lips quirked in a smile, and he saw that her relief outweighed the reservations. "Benjamin really is
my uncle—that's the good news. We've agreed to try
to be friends.''

In gratitude, he bent toward her and kissed her
swiftly on the mouth. "Thank you, Jacqui. I'm sorry
I ever said you were a hard woman. You've done a
wonderful thing today.''

Jacqui smiled at him again and determined to throw
the residue of her doubts into the back corners of her
mind. She relaxed and allowed herself to enjoy everything the moment offered—the warmth of the sun, the
faint hum of insects darting around on the gentle
breeze, the scent of pine, the taste of the food, and
most of all, Zane, who never seemed to be far from
her. He was always as close as a glance or a touch
away.

She wasn't the only one who felt the day was special.
During lunch and afterward, Benjamin radiated good
will and confidence. It was as though, with their confrontation behind him and their tentative new relationship already begun, he felt free to relax the tight
control he'd been exercising over his true nature.

And a powerful nature it was, she acknowledged,
feeling a slight uneasiness as she listened to him relate

yet another anecdote about the fortunes of TMC during the exciting days when uranium mining was in its infancy. She saw the relish for battle in his eyes as he related how he'd fought to maintain control of certain properties; she saw the triumphant flush in his cheeks as he described his eventual victory.

She felt sad. Benjamin had so little of a personal life to show for a lifetime of hard work. From what he'd told her about himself that morning, he was aware that his rough-and-ready personality had been a handicap to him in social situations. His blunt treatment of obstacles had practically guaranteed him a lonely life; people didn't respond well to being maneuvered where they didn't want to go.

Feeling troubled, she let her gaze rest on Zane, who was seated on the ground near her, leaning back against the log she sat on. The tips of his ears reddened as Benjamin launched into a tale that showed Zane in an exceptionally good light.

"Careful, BJ—you make me sound like Zorro."

Benjamin grinned at him. "And so you have been at times, lad. You pulled my neck out of a tight spot that time in Iraq."

Jacqui didn't miss Benjamin's glance at her, checking to see that she was taking it all in. She smiled wryly. Apparently Benjamin believed in nailing down a proposition. He couldn't have made his approval of her new relationship with Zane more obvious.

Something else was obvious, she thought. From Benjamin's remarks about Zane's role in TMC, it seemed clear that Zane was being groomed to take over the company when Benjamin was ready to relinquish the job. Suddenly the enormity of what that meant to her took shape in her mind. Being with Zane up here in the mountains was one thing. What would it be like for them when they returned to the outside world?

I couldn't live the way Zane has to live, she acknowledged to herself, and her inner disturbance mounted. Zane was already deeply involved in a way of life that he admitted was lonely for him. Yet he continued in it, no doubt driven by his loyalty and the debt he owed to Benjamin. *I'm in debt to Benjamin, too,* she reminded herself. It wasn't a very comfortable feeling.

"Jacqui?"

The sound of her name brought her out of her reverie. "I'm sorry, Benjamin. What did you ask me?"

"I was wondering what you're going to do after this summer. Robert told me the other day that your career plans aren't certain."

She collected her scattered thoughts. "I've been torn between my old ideas about working with the Park Service, or teaching. Lately I've come around to the idea that I'd prefer teaching."

"Young children or older ones?" Zane asked.

"The younger ones, I think. A couple of years ago I did some student work with first-graders, and I loved it. They were enthralled by my stories about wilderness creatures. If I can teach children to appreciate such things, maybe offer a regular course in wildlife studies, my teaching might help the next generation take an interest in preserving what we have."

Benjamin said, "You sound like some of the environmental groups that have given my mine managers a good deal of trouble over the years."

"Maybe so, but if we don't treat the subject seriously, all this . . ." She gestured at the clearing and the trees around them. "All this could be gone in our lifetime."

Zane put in, "Jacqui, TMC has had a policy for restoration and reclamation of the land where our mines are located long before government regulations required it."

"I'm glad to hear it." She looked at Zane, aware that he wanted her to think well of Benjamin. His quick defense of her uncle was another reminder of the close bond between the two men.

Benjamin wasn't having it. He said, "I can't take the credit, Jacqui. It was your grandfather's doing. He shamed me into setting up that policy years ago on that trip up the Salmon River. Swore he wouldn't let me go back to civilization until I promised to leave the land as it was before I took out my 'booty.'"

They talked a while longer, then Robert stood up and said, "I have some chores to take care of, so I'd better get started. Jacqui, can I have a word with you?"

"Of course." After a quick glance at Zane, she followed Robert. Once out of earshot of the others, he said abruptly, "Jacqui, I'm worried about this thing between you and Zane. Are you sure you know what you're doing? You've been under a lot of pressure this week, and—"

She laid her hand on his arm. "Rob, I'm sorry. I should have said something to you before this, but I haven't been certain how I felt myself."

"Are you any more sure now? I saw the way you were looking at Zane a minute ago. You didn't look very happy."

She sighed. "All right, I admit some things do worry me. But I care about him, Rob. It may have started out as a crush years ago, but it's very real to me now. Try to understand, and give me your support if you can.''

Robert's frown eased a little, but his voice was still concerned. "I like Zane, Jacqui. And BJ has his good points. But you heard the way he was talking. They come from a world we don't know anything about. They play by rules we probably can't even imagine. I just can't see you living in their world.''

"I can't see me doing that, either, so don't worry too much. That's one of the things I'm going to talk over with Zane as soon as we have the chance.''

When she turned back to find Zane, she was relieved to see that he was alone. As she came up to him, he smiled and said, "Benjamin was more than ready for a nap after his exploits this morning. So we have the afternoon to ourselves, unless Rob wants some more help.''

"Could we go for a walk, Zane? I'd like to talk with you.''

Buddy joined them, and they set off on a path that led uphill, away from the stream. After glancing at her face a time or two, Zane said, "What is it, Jacqui? I've been anxious to hear if BJ was able to answer all your questions this morning.''

"He answered most of them.'' They continued on up the path together, with Buddy bounding off on short side excursions, then forging ahead to disappear for a while. Jacqui related to Zane some of the things Benjamin had told her about her parents' lives and the unfortunate events that led up to the mine explosion.

"Hearing the story from Benjamin's side made me realize how wrong it is to try to put all the blame on one person, the way I blamed Benjamin," she said. "I think he made a mistake trying to force my Dad into a way of life he didn't want. But Dad had his faults, too. I only wanted to remember that he made Mother laugh. I blocked out of my memory that he sometimes made her cry, too."

Zane's hand held hers in a comforting grip. "It's worth a lot that you can face up to that, Jacqui. It's tough to realize that the people who gave us life are only human, like everybody else."

She looked up at him and knew he was thinking of his own parents. Somehow, sometime, he'd come to terms with his past. He'd even forgiven the mother who had abandoned him. Her heart went out to him, and she squeezed his hand tightly.

They came to a halt as the path ended. Huge chunks of granite made a giant's staircase ahead of them. Jacqui said, "It's quite a climb to the top from here, but there's a spectacular view. Do you want to go on?"

He glanced around; this side of the hill opened out on an expansive view of rolling foothills, covered with the multihued shades of green pine and aspen. Below they could see their stream winding and winking through the woods. "This is spectacular enough for me. Let's stop for a while." He lifted her up to sit on a waist-high block of granite, then swung up to sit beside her. He smiled down at her. "This is cosy. Our own private kingdom."

His arm went around her waist, and she rested her head on his shoulder, drawing comfort from his closeness. He said, "Tell me how you came to make a pact of friendship, you and BJ."

She rubbed her cheek against the wool fabric of his sleeve. "I felt sorry for him, Zane. He never deserved the things they said about him—the things *I* said about him, too. But he took it all without a complaint, just to make things easier for Mother and for me. Understanding that makes a lot of difference in the way I feel about the mistakes he made."

She tipped her head up and looked at Zane; with a wry smile she added, "I wonder if you know how strange it feels to realize that I'm confiding my deepest thoughts to a man I could have sworn, only one week ago, I hated."

He lifted his hand and touched the side of her face. "We've come a long way together, Jacqui. This has been an eventful journey for us both, in more ways than one."

"You're right. But it's scary for me. I can't honestly see where it's going to end."

His eyes narrowed, searching her face. "I thought something else was bothering you. Was it something Rob said to you a few minutes ago?"

She shook her head. "He only said some of the same things I've been saying to myself. Zane, you and I haven't looked ahead beyond this week, have we? Our lives are so different. There's my teaching—it's important to me. And your work for Benjamin takes you all over the world for months at a time. When will we have time to be together?"

He turned more toward her, drawing her around until he could see her face clearly. "Jacqui, you said you loved me. That hasn't changed, has it?"

She hesitated, then said, "No, that hasn't changed. But this has all happened too quickly. I don't really know you and you don't know me. And I don't see how we can manage to find the time to remedy that. Once you go back to your field work for TMC—''

He looked relieved. ''That won't be a problem. I plan to cut down the traveling side of my job.''

''How can you do that?''

''Since BJ called me back to the States, I've already started taking on more desk duties. TMC has other troubleshooters; they can take on my travel load.''

''But where will you be stationed? The plans I have for teaching involve my staying in Idaho, at least for another year.''

''I've thought of that, too. We have a regional office in Boise. It wouldn't be too much trouble to switch most of my work there. I figured we could handle other problems if and when they came up.''

Slowly she said, ''That should be okay. But Zane, are you sure you want to make those kinds of changes?''

''Yes, I do.'' His voice was crisp, sure. ''Because we were made to be together, Jacqui. I can see you need a little more time to feel as certain as I do. I love you— and that's something I've never told any woman before.''

He kissed her then, and she felt that he was trying to say with his lips and hands and body the things he'd said in words. Her heart seemed to swell inside her breast in an upsurge of emotion that pushed her doubts back into the shadows. With a soundless sigh of acceptance, she gave herself up to the dizzying spiral of feeling he roused in her. The sun-warmed stone they sat on might as well have been fluffy clouds, because she scarcely felt the uneven hardness as their bodies strained for closeness. With her arms wrapped around his shoulders, her fingers tangled in his hair, she gave herself up to the magic.

When the kiss finally ended, she held on to him tightly, wanting the moment to go on forever. *Up here, anything seems possible. If only I could hold on to this feeling...*

She put her yearning into words. "Zane, it will work between us, won't it? I want it to, so terribly much."

His eyes were dark with feeling as he kissed her again and said, "We'll make it work, I promise you."

When they returned to camp, Jacqui saw Robert near the supply tent. To Zane, she said, "I want to talk to Rob for a minute. He's concerned for me, and I don't want him to worry."

He nodded. "Good idea. I'll talk to him myself, later."

She didn't beat around the bush. "Rob, I've talked to Zane. He says he's going to quit traveling and settle down in Boise where I can teach. We're going to work things out. I'm sure of that now."

"I hope so, Jacqui."

"He wants to talk to you. Rob, I do want you to be friends. He's never had any family. I'd like him to feel he has one with us."

Robert grinned at her sheepishly. "Well, I hope he doesn't start by asking me for my blessing. I'm not very good at this sort of thing. All I care about is for you to be happy."

A few minutes later the two men went off together, ostensibly to see about moving the horses to a new grazing area. Jacqui started preparing their evening meal, wondering what Zane would be saying to Robert. Immersed in her thoughts, she had to muster up a smile when Benjamin came out of his tent and approached the kitchen area.

"You're looking well, BJ," she said. "I'm glad to see our mountain air has been good for you."

"It's you and Zane who've been good for me," he said. He took a seat on the stump where he'd sat earlier, cleaning the fish. "I'm very happy for you both, Jacqui. It's more than I ever dared dream, for you two to get together."

She couldn't help wishing Benjamin weren't quite so ready to talk about a subject that was still intensely personal to her. She gave him a brief smile and knelt to dig out a skillet from the stack of kitchen supplies.

He wasn't deterred by her lack of response. Leaning forward, he braced his hands on his knees and said, "I'm glad to get this chance to talk with you. We need to make some plans. How serious are you about that teaching job you mentioned, come this fall?"

"Very serious. Why?"

"Well, it's like this... I'd like you to put off those plans, Jacqui. When you and Zane get married, you'll have some big changes to deal with."

"We haven't actually spoken of marriage yet, BJ." She was holding the skillet in midair, staring at him. Now she set down the pan with great care.

He made a dismissing gesture with one hand. "Of course you'll get married. Zane is an honorable man; he wouldn't think of offering my niece anything but marriage. The thing is, my dear, it's a big job running TMC. I have some good men running the various divisions, but my company needs a strong hand at the helm. Zane has what it takes to carry on when I finally let go of the reins, but you're my only heir, along

with him. I want you to have a say in running the
business, too.''

She stared at him blankly. ''Benjamin, that's impossible. I don't know the first thing about running a
corporation.''

''I know your training has been in a different field.
But you're a Treherne; you're smart and you have
common sense. Your stepbrother told me how you
helped him set up his guide business. I'm sure that in
a couple of years, with me teaching you what you need
to know and Zane handling the tough calls, you'll
make a top-notch executive.''

''But I'm not interested in—''

He seemed to be looking inward at some private vision that gave him a great deal of satisfaction. As
though speaking to himself, he went on, ''You'll
probably want to travel a good deal at first, to get the
feel of the business. London, Paris, South America—
you'll enjoy that part of it. I always regretted not being
able to give you a chance to see more of the world.''
He focused on her again, and she saw his enthusiasm.
''What do you say to my proposition, Jacqui?''

Remember TMC is his whole life, she cautioned
herself. *He thinks he's offering you a wonderful opportunity.* She took in a deep breath. ''I have to say
no, Benjamin. I've told you—I work with animals, I
teach. There's absolutely no reason for me to take any
part in your business affairs.''

His smile at her was kindly. ''I understand that the
idea is new to you. But you'll have to learn how to
handle TMC someday. I hate to admit it, but Zane is
right; my health isn't what it should be. There may not
be much time to see you settled in. I have to make sure
you'll be all right.''

It took a tremendous effort not to say all that was teeming inside her. She had a sudden vision of the life he was planning for her. TMC was worth millions...more. With Zane at her side, wrapped up in running the business, their lives would be affected at every turn by Benjamin, advising, controlling... Her blood chilled in her veins and her old feelings about her uncle rushed up within her. Robert had been right to urge her to be cautious. However well-meaning Benjamin might be, he was a threat to anyone coming within range of his money, his power. Had her father felt that power, too, and tried to run from it?

She felt a flash of panic and raised her hand as though to ward off a danger. "No, Benjamin—you can't just step into my life and take it over. I won't let you. God, no wonder my mother wouldn't let you near us after Dad died."

No sooner had the words passed her lips than she regretted them, but it was too late. Benjamin looked as though she'd struck him. Distressed, she amended, "No—I'm sorry I said that. But please get this straight, Benjamin. I don't *want* what you're offering me. I know it means a great deal to you, but I'm sorry—I just don't want it." She spun on her heel and hurried off, almost bumping into Zane and Robert as they returned to camp.

Zane called out, "Jacqui? Where are you going?"

Too upset to stop, even for Zane, she grabbed a blanket and bridle and ran most of the way to the clearing where the horses were grazing. She'd just whistled for the gelding when Zane caught up with her. "Where on earth are you going? The sun's almost down; in another hour you won't be able to see your hand in front of your face."

"I have to get away—I've got to think." Agitation made her fingers clumsy, but she slipped the bridle into place over the gelding's head and secured it. "I'll camp out in the woods by myself. I've done it often enough before."

"With nothing but a blanket, and no supplies?" He grasped her arm, preventing her mounting. "For God's sake, tell me what happened back there—what did BJ say to put you in this state?"

It was the urgency in his voice rather than his hand on her arm that stopped her. She felt a tremor deep inside, and for a moment she sagged against the horse's side. Then she straightened and turned around. "Zane, it's not going to work. I just can't handle this."

Zane's face looked pale. "What are you talking about?"

In an uneven voice she said, "Benjamin has my future all organized for me. You and I are to be married, and we're to run TMC after he's gone. He plans to train me himself, so I can handle my share of his fortune."

"Lord, Jacqui—"

She was shivering and couldn't seem to stop. "Zane, I can't take his interfering in our lives. And he will. I don't think he can help it."

Zane put his arms around her and drew her close. "Shh, darling—we can handle it. Give him time to adjust. In the end, it's you and me who have the final say. I won't let him run our lives."

She shook her head, unable to draw comfort from his words. "You owe him so much, Zane. He really cares about you, I know he does. And he means well by me, too. How can I fight against that? But I have to—I won't be swallowed up by him!''

"Jacqui, we can work it out—"

She pushed away from him. "Maybe. But I think we need more time before we make any firm commitments, Zane. I care about you, very much. But I'm not sure caring will be enough to stand up against the strain of wondering what he's going to do next. Maybe I'm paranoid about this, but—"

"Jacqui ... Zane ..." A voice called to them from the edge of the clearing, a few feet away. Startled, they both looked over and saw Benjamin standing next to one of the trees, his hand braced on the trunk. "I'm sorry, Jacqui. I didn't mean to upset you. I only wanted what I thought was best for you. I'm a blind, bullheaded fool—forgive me, please."

He stumbled as he moved toward them, and Jacqui cried out. "Zane, catch him—he's going to fall!"

They both reached him just before he crumpled. Zane's face was stiff with anxiety as he cradled Benjamin's shoulders and eased him to the ground. "Quick, in his breast pocket—his pills!"

Jacqui knelt and found the small bottle and handed it to Zane. She watched him slip a tablet under Benjamin's tongue. The old man's eyes were closed, the color of his lips bluish. "Is ... is he going to ...?"

"Die?" Zane's reply was abrupt, almost harsh. "No, I hope not. Will you stay with him while I run back to camp? Robert can radio the helicopter service in Sun Valley. They should be here in less than an hour, if they're on the job."

"But it'll be dark soon. They won't be able to land," she protested.

He was already transferring Benjamin's shoulders and head into her lap, very carefully. "We can set up signal fires around the clearing here. There's room enough for a landing, even in the dark."

She looked up at him, searching his face. Did he blame her for Benjamin's attack? His tight expression brought her no comfort as he rose briskly and said, "I'll bring back blankets and a light. Stay put and be sure to keep his head and upper body elevated."

He started running back toward camp. Jacqui was left alone with Benjamin. In the gathering twilight, only the sound of his stertorous breathing broke the silence. Inside she felt a steadily growing remorse and fear. What if Benjamin should die? In the heat of the moment, she'd forgotten about his heart condition. She bowed her head and let the slow tears trickle down her cheeks.

Chapter Ten

The helicopter hovered like some great wing-flapping bird of the night before settling gently into the clearing in the minor whirlwind of its own creating. Four widely spaced bonfires gave off a reddish glow that only partially relieved the darkness.

Jacqui tended Benjamin, now well wrapped in blankets to ward off shock. She watched Zane's face as he waited for the paramedics to alight from the helicopter. In the flickering light of a signal fire, his face, starkly shadowed, seemed like the face of a stranger.

With swift competence, the paramedics soon had Benjamin installed on a stretcher, and the stretcher tucked into the body of the helicopter. Zane turned to Jacqui and asked, "You'll be going back to Ketchum in the morning?"

Her throat felt too tight for speech. She nodded, and he said, "I'll call you when I can."

He ducked his head and climbed into the cockpit. It
was only after the aircraft had lifted off and whirled
away into the night that she regained her voice.
"Godspeed," she whispered. She dug her hands into
the pockets of her windbreaker and took what comfort she could when Robert came up beside her and
silently put his arm around her shoulders.

At dawn the next morning, they packed everything
up for the return trip. Buddy seemed to sense their
glum mood, and stayed out of their way. He watched
them solemnly with golden eyes that seemed almost
sympathetic. Jacqui stopped briefly to pat him. "It
does feel strange not having Zane here, doesn't it,
Buddy? I miss him, too."

She looked around the camp. Dawn was gradually
turning everything from gray to the bright hues of
morning, but she felt drained and bleak inside. *I never
used to cry,* she thought as she picked up the last bundle of supplies, ready to load on the packhorse. *So
why did I cry so much last night after they'd gone? For
Benjamin? Or for myself, because whatever chance
Zane and I might have had probably ended last night?*

Robert, leading up the packhorse, caught her wip-
ing tears from her cheek with the back of her hand.
She felt his arm come around her shoulders in a comforting hug. He said, "Don't worry, Jacqui. It will all
work out."

She looked up at him. "Do you really think so,
Rob? It seems to me that this trip has turned out to be
a disaster."

"It could have been a lot worse. We were lucky
Zane had laid on emergency service. And the helicopter pilot told me they wouldn't have risked a night
flight if we were any higher up on the trail."

"I hope Benjamin made it all right. It's terrible knowing I'm at least partly responsible for his attack." She'd already told Robert what had happened the previous evening.

Now he gave her a quick hug in sympathy and asked, "How do you feel this morning about BJ saying those things to you?"

She moved away, frowning unhappily. "He took me by surprise. I'd only just gotten used to the idea of being friendly, and suddenly he had me sitting behind a desk at TMC! I wanted out, and I overreacted. I didn't even think about him being ill. I'll never forgive myself if he dies. And I suspect Zane won't forgive me, either."

Robert patted her shoulder awkwardly. "Well, we can't do anything up here. Let's get cracking down the trail. We can be home before nightfall if we take the short route back. Zane said they were taking BJ to the hospital in Boise. You can call when we get home to find out how he is."

"Yes." Her voice choked. "Or whether he made it at all. Let's ride, Rob!"

The steady hum-click noise of the heart-monitoring machine beside Benjamin's bed provided a reassuring note amid the bustling sounds in the cardiac ward at Boise Medical Center. Zane sat in a chair near the head of Benjamin's bed, leaning forward, resting his forearms on his thighs.

They'd been in time. The transfer to the hospital after their swift helicopter ride last night had gone without a hitch. When Zane had walked into the intensive-care ward, the nurses had started to order him out, but after a quiet word from Benjamin's doctor, they'd allowed him to stay. The long hours of watching and waiting had given Zane plenty of time to think. Earlier that morning, Benjamin had been awake and had groggily asserted himself by demanding to know just how long he was going to be kept tied into his bed. He'd insisted on having the protective strapping removed at once. The nurse, after one shrewd look at him, had agreed on condition that he settle down and not try to get out of bed under any circumstances. Grumbling, he'd subsided, then smiled at Zane weakly. "Got to keep them on their toes, lad. Otherwise they run right over you."

Benjamin was sleeping now, but Zane continued his vigil. He propped his head in his hands. Lord, he was tired. His entire body ached. He'd managed to wash off some of the smoke-black from the fires they'd built to guide the helicopter in, but he knew he still looked like a commando just back from a rough mission.

He looked over at the sleeping face of the man who'd been his employer, friend and the closest thing to a father that he'd ever know, and wondered how he was going to tell him about the decision he'd come to, somewhere in the early hours of the morning. *BJ will understand,* he told himself. *But God, I hate to hurt him any more than he's been hurt already.*

His planning might be wasted, anyway. Both he and Benjamin had pushed Jacqui too far and too fast. For a while, he'd allowed himself to believe she'd thrown off the bonds of the past. But it was possible she couldn't—that the scars went too deep.

Zane pressed his knuckles into his forehead, trying to ease the dull ache there. He heard the rustle of the cubicle's curtain and sighed inwardly. He'd hoped there would be a respite from the nurses for a while; BJ had only fallen asleep again a short while ago.

"Zane?"

His head jerked up. It took him a second to recognize Jacqui out of her trail gear. She was now wearing a green linen blouse and skirt, her hair loose around her shoulders.

"Jacqui?" He started to his feet.

"The nurse said I could come in for just a moment. If it's all right with you?"

Looking closer, he saw the blue smudges beneath her eyes, the paleness of her cheeks; she hadn't slept, either. He reached for her elbow to steer her to the only chair in the cubicle. "Yes, of course it's all right," he said in the same low tone she'd used. "Sit down here. BJ is asleep."

Jacqui felt a pang of concern as her gaze took in Zane's red-rimmed eyes and the dark stubble on his face. Then she turned her eyes toward the bed, almost dreading what she'd see there. Her heart sank as she saw how frail Benjamin looked, how pale, his white hair hardly distinguishable from the whiteness of the pillow beneath his head. He looked so different from the smiling, genial man she'd come to know during the past week. She whispered, "Is he all right, Zane? I called last night, but they wouldn't tell me anything except that he was doing as well as could be expected. I drove down this morning as soon as I could."

"He's going to be okay, this time." Zane, standing behind her chair, pressed her shoulder reassuringly. "An hour or so ago he was awake and fussing at the nurses. You should have heard him."

She reached up to grip Zane's hand. "I wish I had heard. Maybe then I could believe he's really going to get better." Her voice caught, then she added, "Zane, I'm so sorry..."

"Hey, what's going on around here? Are you two starting the wake without me?" The voice from the bed was weak, but carried a familiar humorous tone. Benjamin's eyes were open, and he was looking at Jacqui. "I'm not ready to go just yet, my dear."

Tears sprang into her eyes. When he reached out his hand, hesitantly, she took it gently into hers and said, "I'm very happy to hear that. I'm not ready for you to go, either."

He managed a grin. "Because you don't want to get saddled with the old man's empire? Don't worry about that, Jacqui. I was out of line trying to set up everything for you... without making sure it was what you wanted. I'm sorry."

He was out of breath when he finished speaking. Jacqui was conscious of Zane's hand squeezing her shoulder as she smiled at her uncle. "It's all right. I'm sorry I said what I did to you. I spoke without thinking."

"We'll do better next time?"

She squeezed his hand gently. "We'll do better. But you'll have to promise to get well first. You're the only uncle I've got, remember." His fingers tightened on hers and she saw that he was too moved to speak.

The curtains swished back and the head nurse stood looking at them disapprovingly. "I think Mr. Treherne will do better if he rests quietly for a while." Her suggestion sounded more like a command.

Zane looked down at Benjamin and grasped his hand briefly. "We'll be back later, BJ. I think you'd better not try to push this nurse around."

Benjamin's feeble chuckle followed them as they left.

Outside the cardiac ward, Zane said, "Let's go outside. I can't breathe in here anymore."

Boise Medical Center was not the same hospital where her mother had spent her last hours, but Jacqui had a feeling of déjà vu as Zane guided her down the corridor and into the elevator that would take them to the ground floor. The only difference was that this time it was Zane's eyes that were red-rimmed and tired. He looked exhausted. And he still hadn't said a single personal word to her. Her heart sank.

Once outside the hospital, the heat and glare from sidewalks and concrete buildings hit them. A bus's engine roared at a nearby curb. Cars passed in the street, adding to the clamor of city sounds. Jacqui heard Zane take in a sharp breath. He said, "Not much like the green forest and mountains we left a few hours ago, is it? Are your shoes okay for walking? I feel like I'll explode if I don't get moving."

"I feel the same way." They set off, and Jacqui had reason to be glad of her long legs and the flared fit of her skirt. Zane set a good pace. She welcomed the exercise; the hours she'd spent cramped in the front seat of her car had taken its toll on her, too. They must have covered ten blocks before she finally stopped him in front of a small café on a quiet street. "Zane, how long has it been since you had anything to eat? I'll bet you haven't had a thing except coffee."

He rubbed his hand around the back of his neck and nodded. "You're right about that."

"Let's go in here and have something, then." She steered him inside, and soon they were settled at a table covered with a bright checked cloth and a vase of perky-looking daisies. The waitress took their order and bustled away. Appetizing smells came from the kitchen in the back. Only one other table in the café was occupied.

Zane slid down in his seat and closed his eyes. "It's nice and quiet here. The noise never stopped in the hospital." He opened his eyes suddenly and looked at her, then said abruptly, "It was a long night."

She nodded. "Yes, it was. But at least BJ will be all right."

"You didn't say anything when I left on the helicopter. Not even goodbye."

Zane's tone sounded faintly accusing, and Jacqui answered defensively. "I couldn't. I felt terrible. I thought you might be blaming me for what happened to Benjamin."

His eyes narrowed. "Of course I didn't blame you. Why do you think I would?"

"Because I overreacted when he told me what he had in mind for me, and I said something cruel. If I hadn't gotten so upset with him, he might not have had the attack."

Zane shook his head. "It was bound to happen, sooner or later. Now maybe he'll give in and have the operation he needs. What you said to him today will give him a good reason to have it done."

"Then I'm glad I said it." Seeing him frown, she paused. "Is there something you're not telling me?"

He shrugged. "I'm not sure you realize what you've let yourself in for. You've just about committed yourself to keeping up relations with BJ."

"Yes, I do realize that. I—"

The waitress came up just then, bearing plates of food. She slid the plates in front of them, saying, "Here you are, folks—pancakes with hot syrup, o.j., eggs and sausages. Are you sure you don't want coffee?"

Jacqui said, "No thanks, the orange juice will be fine." She glanced across the table and saw that Zane was moodily contemplating his food. Her throat constricted, and she thought, *At another time, he would have looked at me and we would have shared a smile because we both know coffee is the last thing we want right now. Now we can't even smile together.*

Zane picked up his fork and said, "We'd better eat. I don't want to stay away from the hospital too long. BJ's doctor will be making his rounds soon."

Jacqui tried to eat, but after a few bites gave up. "Zane, a minute ago you sounded like you thought I might not mean what I said to BJ."

He stabbed a piece of sausage with his fork and ate it before he said, "I've been thinking, Jacqui. You've carried some very strong feelings against BJ over the years. It may not be possible for you to throw them off completely. You've had a lot asked of you in a very short time. I can hardly blame you for deciding it was too much after BJ tried to get you involved in TMC."

The unhappy aching in her breast increased. Why was Zane behaving so coolly toward her, saying things that put her at a distance? If he'd had second thoughts about his involvement with her, why didn't he tell her?

She forced herself to deal with what he'd actually said. "I meant what I said to him. I admit I didn't want to go on the trip, but a lot has changed since we started up into the mountains. Benjamin is my uncle.

Whatever faults he has, he is my father's brother—and I owe him something for all those years I treated him so badly.''

Zane's expression still gave her no clue to his feelings. Watching her intently, he said, "I've noticed that whenever you speak about BJ, there's always a touch of reserve in your voice. And you mention his faults. It makes me think that nothing he could do would ever change the way you really feel about him, in your heart.''

She looked back at him in helpless frustration. Zane was looking and speaking to her now with such detachment that she wondered how she could tell him what was in her heart—that she'd mainly come to fear Benjamin's interference in their lives as a couple? Her parents' marriage hadn't survived, and she didn't want to see history repeat itself. But she'd sound like a fool if she brought that up as a reason now. Any kind of relationship between them seemed extremely remote.

Zane exhaled sharply, tossed his napkin on the table and sat back. He looked more tired than ever. Heavily he said, "I'd hoped we could work something out. But I guess you've had enough of both BJ and me.''

Now it was her turn to frown. "What are you talking about? What do you mean, had enough?''

"Aren't you trying to come up with a tactful way of saying it won't work between us? That you made a mistake?''

"What on earth gave you that idea? You're the one who's cooled off—you haven't said a personal word to me since I came down here.''

They looked at each other with mixed feelings beginning to show on their faces. "We seem to be talking at cross purposes here," Zane said.

"Then you haven't changed your mind about... about us?"

As though revitalized, Zane leaned forward across the table. "Lord, no. I thought you had."

A smile began in the corners of her mouth and spread outward. "Zane, we've been very foolish."

He grinned at her and suddenly his eyes were anything but unrevealing. They were alight with feelings that started her pulse rioting in response. "We've been prime idiots." He shoved their plates aside, then reached for her hands and gripped them tightly. "Jacqui, once I knew BJ was going to be all right, I spent the rest of the night trying to figure how we could work things out, in case you couldn't get along with him."

She gripped his hands back just as tightly. "I didn't say I couldn't get along with him. I'm just afraid he won't let us live our own lives. TMC means so much to him, and he wants us to run it. And I don't think I could live that way."

"You don't have to worry about that. As soon as he's fit again—and he will be if he has that operation—he'll be back watching over every step of TMC business himself. It'll be a long time before he's ready to let go of the reins." Zane's smile tilted at her again. "I seem to remember you telling me that I was good enough to find work anywhere, or to start up a business of my own."

"You mean you'd leave TMC?" Astonished, she stared at him.

He nodded. "I don't mean that I wouldn't see BJ—and often. He's more than just an employer to me. But working for him takes a full-time commitment, and my first commitment now is to you. I don't want either one of you getting hurt. But if it's a choice of protecting one or the other of you from getting hurt, it's you that I have to protect. Because I love you—you're the other part of me. I can't do without you."

She could see he meant every word. Deeply moved, she said, "It means a great deal to me that you feel that way. I think we can work things out with BJ so he won't be hurt, either. He needs to feel like he's a part of a family, too. He—"

She broke off, and felt a quick rush of color to her cheeks. "Listen to me. I'm talking like everything is settled. We haven't even—"

Zane reached out and covered her hand with his. The light in his eyes grew brighter. "That's the next thing we have to talk about. But let's head back to the hospital first. We should be where BJ's doctor can get hold of us if he needs to."

Outside the café, Zane hailed a cab and they were soon back at the hospital. Along the way, Jacqui marveled at the amazing turn of events during the brief space of half an hour. From dreading that Zane was ready to call it quits to suddenly making plans for a real commitment—it was almost too much! And by telling her of his scheme to alter his work just so they could protect what they had together, he'd shown her in the most effective way possible that he truly *did* care for her. She felt tears come into her eyes.

They checked in with the nurse's station in intensive care, and Zane left word that they could be found in the plaza behind the main building. Then he guided

Jacqui through the maze of doors and corridors until they stepped outside again, this time into a small outdoor garden. It was no more than a concrete expanse with benches and boxes containing shrubs and flowers, but it was a sunny spot, and best of all, it was deserted.

"I found this place last night," he said. "I walked here for a bit and thought about you. Jacqui—" His voice had deepened with feeling. Suddenly he swept her into his arms. He held her tightly, his face buried in the softness of her hair at the side of her neck. She felt a tremor run through his body, and she hugged him back as hard as she could, sensing his need for closeness. A wave of love passed over her, so strong it was almost painful.

Finally his tight grip slackened. He exhaled, then lifted his head to smile wearily at her. "It feels so good to have you in my arms. I feel like I've been starving for you. When that helicopter took off last night, I could hardly bear to leave you behind. I can't do without you now."

She reached up and touched the side of his face, felt the roughness of his unshaved cheek, delighting in the sensation. Dreamily she said, "Zane, do you know when I first knew I was falling in love with you? For real, I mean?"

He tilted his head and rubbed his face gently against her hand, as though savoring the intimacy of her touch. "When was that?"

"That day after we fell in the lake, when you were shaving under a tree. We were out in the middle of the wilderness, and the mirror from your shaving kit was perched on the limb of a tree, but somehow it seemed so homey, so right. I stood there watching you, and I knew I wanted to go on sharing moments like that with you for the rest of my life.''

He gave her a wry grin. "But you didn't let me know that. In fact, you warned me a minute later to keep my distance."

She shook her head ruefully. "I was really mixed up. I just couldn't believe my feelings about you could change so fast."

"It happened even faster for me. As soon as I saw you walking down the street in Ketchum, the six years we were separated went up in a puff of smoke. I wanted you more than ever."

A laugh bubbled up in her throat. "You hid your feelings very well. When you told me how hardhearted I was, I was certain you despised me."

"That was purely defensive. I was afraid you'd tilt that stubborn chin, look at me with those scornful eyes, and tell me to go to hell. Which is exactly what you did."

"I did, didn't I? Well, you shouldn't have tried to blackmail me. That was a bit hard to take."

"Here, let's sit down." He led her over to a long wooden bench in one corner. When they were settled, with Jacqui comfortably nestled against his side, he wrapped his arms more securely around her and said, "About that blackmail... At the time, I was at the end of my rope. The look you gave me was plenty of punishment, though. I felt like a complete heel."

"Well, I suppose I'll have to forgive you. I was pretty stubborn. I was determined to block out everything to do with the past, and you wouldn't let me."

His hand cupped under her chin, tilted her head so he could look at her directly. "I couldn't—not just because it shut me out, too, but for your own sake.

Blocking out the past doesn't work; you have to re-solve it first.''

"You're talking from experience, aren't you?"

He nodded. "There was a time when I used to pre-tend that my folks had just left me behind temporari-ly, that they'd come back for me someday. It wasn't easy to let go of that, to accept the fact that I was on my own.''

"You were so young. Where did you get the cour-age?''

"Where did you get yours, Sister Wolf?"

The blazing look of love in his eyes took away her capabilities of speech. *He's reaching out to me,* she thought. *He's holding nothing back—he's sharing everything with me. How rare it is for two people to have that . . . and how wonderful.*

"I used to think your eyes were so unrevealing," she said when she could speak again. She reached up to touch his temple where dark hair, unruly now, curled toward his brow. She stroked the soft strands back, and went on, "And sometimes they do hide what you're thinking. But now I can look right through them—see inside you.''

"Jacqui . . . my love . . .'' Emotion made his voice thick. She felt an equal outpouring of feeling too in-tense for words. Clumsily, almost blindly, their lips met, their arms strained to make the embrace closer. Deep inside herself, Jacqui felt as though she were flying without wings, soaring into a new world, and she was not alone.

It was a long time before they came down to earth again, and even longer before their feelings calmed enough to speak. Resting her cheek against his chest, hearing the heavy thud of his heartbeat, breathing in

the smoky scent of his clothes, Jacqui felt gloriously
content. She chuckled.

"What's funny?" he asked, and she heard the smile
in his voice. His fingers played with her hair, sending
prickles of delightful sensation down her spine.

"You smell of wood smoke and maybe a little bit of
horse," she said. "Poor darling, you haven't had a
minute to yourself since last night, have you?"

The arm around her waist slackened, and he looked
from her fresh clothes to his crumpled, dirty ones.
"Jacqui, I never thought. I'm getting you all messed
up, too. I need to check into a motel and get cleaned
up."

She wouldn't let him draw away from her. "Oh, no
you don't. Do you think I care about a spot or two on
my clothes? We've gone far beyond that, Zane. We've
seen each other at our worst this past week. I know
what you look like in the morning with your face all
covered with shaving cream, and you know what I
look like when I'm wringing wet and covered with
mud. I'd say we've had an unorthodox courtship,
wouldn't you?"

She felt the rise and fall of his chest as he laughed.
He touched her cheek, then said in a different tone,
"You may be right that our courtship hasn't been or-
thodox. I used to dream that one day, if I found the
right woman, I'd do it right."

She pulled away enough to look directly at him, her
brow puckering. "I wasn't complaining, Zane. I—"

"No, hear me out, please. I want you to know just
what you're getting into with me." Looking deep into
her eyes, he said huskily, "I want to be your lover,
your mate. I want us to have a long life together—
good times and bad, whatever comes our way. I want

to see my ring on your finger, and yours on mine. I would be honored if you would be my wife, Jacqui."

Surprised and deeply moved by his formal proposal, she gave him a shaky smile and answered in kind. "I would be honored to be your wife, Zane. I'll wear your ring and give you mine, but I won't need a ring to remind me of the pledge I'm making you now, or the love I feel for you."

They fell silent, and the echo of their exchanged vows seemed to shimmer in the air. *I'll never forget this little concrete garden,* Jacqui thought. Joy sang inside her, and she said, "Zane, you know what you told me in Sun Valley, when I insisted we'd be saying goodbye at the end of the trek? You said it would be just the beginning for us."

"Yes, I remember." He was smiling, his gaze wandering over her face, lingering on her lips.

"Well, you were right." Her hand slid up over his strong shoulders to curve around his neck, to draw him closer. "This is just the beginning for us, my darling. And you'll have to wait a long, long time to hear me say goodbye."

"Like how long?" His mouth brushed hers, his lips parted.

"Like forever."

And then their lips met and they forgot the past, the future and everything else except the excitement of the present.

* * * * *

Silhouette Desire ®

1989
IS THE YEAR
OF THE MAN!

What makes a romance? A special man, of course, and Silhouette Desire celebrates that fact with *twelve* of them! From Mr. January to Mr. December, every month has a tribute to the Silhouette Desire hero—our **MAN OF THE MONTH!**

Sexy, macho, charming, irritating . . . irresistible! Nothing can stop these men from sweeping you away. Created by some of your favorite authors, each man is custom-made for pleasure—*reading* pleasure—so don't miss a single one.

Mr. January is Blake Donavan in RELUCTANT FATHER by Diana Palmer
Mr. February is Hank Branson in THE GENTLEMAN INSISTS by Joan Hohl
Mr. March is Carson Tanner in NIGHT OF THE HUNTER by Jennifer Greene
Mr. April is Slater McCall in A DANGEROUS KIND OF MAN by Naomi Horton
Mr. May is Luke Harmon in VENGEANCE IS MINE by Lucy Gordon
Mr. June is Quinn McNamara in IRRESISTIBLE by Annette Broadrick

And that's only the half of it—
so get out there and find your man!

Silhouette Desire's

MAN OF THE MONTH . . .

MOM-1

Silhouette Classics

COMING IN APRIL...

THORNE'S WAY by Joan Hohl

When *Thorne's Way* first burst upon the romance scene in 1982, readers couldn't help but fall in love with Jonas Thorne, a man of bewildering arrogance and stunning tenderness. This book quickly became one of Silhouette's most sought-after early titles.

Now, Silhouette Classics is pleased to present the reissue of *Thorne's Way*. Even if you read this book years ago, its depth of emotion and passion will stir your heart again and again.

And that's not all!

Silhouette Special Edition

COMING IN JULY...

THORNE'S WIFE by Joan Hohl

We're pleased to announce a truly unique event at Silhouette. Jonas Thorne is back, in *Thorne's Wife*, a sequel that will sweep you off your feet! Jonas and Valerie's story continues as life—and love—reach heights never before dreamed of.

Experience both these timeless classics—one from Silhouette Classics and one from Silhouette Special Edition—as master storyteller Joan Hohl weaves two passionate, dramatic tales of everlasting love!

Silhouette Special Edition®

NAVY BLUES
Debbie Macomber

Between the devil and the deep blue sea...

At Christmastime, Lieutenant Commander Steve Kyle finds his heart anchored by the past, so he vows to give his ex-wife wide berth. But Carol Kyle is quaffing milk and knitting tiny pastel blankets with a vengeance. She's determined to have a baby, and only one man will do as father-to-be—the only man she's ever loved...her own bullheaded ex-husband!

You met Steve and Carol in NAVY WIFE (Special Edition #494)—you'll cheer for them in NAVY BLUES (Special Edition #518). (And as a bonus for NAVY WIFE fans, newlyweds Rush and Lindy Callaghan reveal a surprise of their own....)

Each book stands alone—together they're Debbie Macomber's most delightful duo to date! Don't miss

NAVY BLUES
Available in April,
only in *Silhouette Special Edition*.
Having the "blues" was never
so much fun!

SE518-1A

You'll flip . . . your pages won't!
Read paperbacks *hands-free* with

Book Mate · I

The perfect "mate" for all your romance paperbacks

Traveling • Vacationing • At Work • In Bed • Studying
• Cooking • Eating

Perfect size for all standard paperbacks, this wonderful invention makes reading a pure pleasure! Ingenious design holds paperback books OPEN and FLAT so even wind can't ruffle pages — leaves your hands free to do other things. Reinforced, wipe-clean vinyl-covered holder flexes to let you turn pages without undoing the strap . . . supports paperbacks so well, they have the strength of hardcovers!

Pages turn WITHOUT opening the strap.

SEE-THROUGH STRAP

Reinforced back stays flat.

Built in bookmark.

BOOK MARK

BACK COVER HOLDING STRIP

10" x 7¼", opened.
Snaps closed for easy carrying, too.

Silhouette Intimate Moments®

Let Bestselling Author KATHLEEN EAGLE Sweep You Away to De Colores Once Again

For the third time, Kathleen Eagle has written a book set on the spellbinding isle of De Colores. In PAINTBOX MORNING (Intimate Moments #284), Miguel Hidalgo is all that stands between his island home and destruction—and Ronnie Harper is the only woman who can help Miguel fulfill his destiny and lead his people into a bright tomorrow. But Ronnie has a woman's heart, a woman's needs. In helping Miguel to live out his dreams, is she destined to see her own dreams of love with this very special man go forever unfulfilled? Read PAINTBOX MORNING, coming this month from Silhouette Intimate Moments, and follow the path of these star-crossed lovers as they build a future filled with hope and a love to last all time.

If you like PAINTBOX MORNING, you might also like Kathleen Eagle's two previous tales of De Colores: CANDLES IN THE NIGHT (Special Edition #437) and MORE THAN A MIRACLE (Intimate Moments #242).
